THE REBECCA RIOTER

A Story of Killay Life

by

AMY DILLWYN

with an introduction by

KATIE GRAMICH

HONNO CLASSICS

Published by Honno
'Alisa Craig', Heol y Cawl, Dinas Powys
South Glamorgan, Wales, CF6 4AH

First Impression 1880
This edition © Honno Ltd 2001

© Introduction Katie Gramich 2001

British Library Cataloguing in Publication Data

ISBN 1 870206 43 6

Published with the financial support of the Arts Council of Wales.

Cover: A portrait of Amy Dillwyn, courtesy of David Painting.

Cover design by Chris Lee Design

Typeset and printed in Wales by
Gwasg Dinefwr, Llandybïe

Introduction

AMY DILLWYN
A brief biography

Elizabeth Amy Dillwyn was born in Swansea in 1845, two years after the actual attack on the Pontardulais Turnpike by Rebecca Rioters which forms the central event in her novel. As the opening pages of *The Rebecca Rioter* make clear, this is a narrative which looks back on the events of a generation before. Amy Dillwyn acts the part of the ventriloquist in making her narrator one of the rioters, and her story is a rewriting of the account given by her own father, Lewis Llewelyn Dillwyn, who had been both an eye-witness and a participant in the struggle with the rioters, recording his experiences in a handwritten memorandum. Amy's novel can be viewed variously in relation to her father's still extant narrative: as a sequel, a fictionalisation, a tribute, an imitation, or, as I shall argue, a radical rewriting and an act of filial defiance, with a feminist twist.

Amy, like her alter ego in the novel, Gwenllian Tudor, had a privileged upbringing as a member of a wealthy family of industrialists and politicians. Despite some aristocratic pretensions, this was a nouveau riche family with interestingly contradictory origins, namely on the one side Quakers who had supported slave emancipation and on the other West India plantation owners. Unsurprisingly, perhaps, there were elements of unconventionality and radicalism in the family even before Amy herself came to prominence. Both her grandfathers were fundamentally Victorian scientists, whose main love was for geology and botany, though they had to make their far from paltry living from business (the Cambrian pottery) and politics. Her father was something of a radical who became Liberal MP in Swansea in 1855 largely on the grounds of his religious tolerance (the erstwhile Quakers had in the previous generation joined the Anglican Church in Wales but Dillwyn's liberal views appealed to what was in effect a 'nation of Nonconformists'). The third of four children, including an older brother and two sisters, Amy was brought up in comfort firstly in a large house called Parkwern, near her grandparents' mansion, Sketty Hall, and later in Hendrefoilan House, a grand edifice built by her father in anticipation of his new role as the local member of parliament.

In the Autumn of 1863, after 'coming out' in London as every good debutante must, Amy became engaged to Llewellyn Thomas of Llwynmadoc, a young man of wealthy, landowning stock whom she had known for most of her life. Sadly, only four months after the engagement, Llewellyn died of smallpox. Given the small number of bachelors deemed eligible, particularly by the exacting Amy, it looked likely from then on that she would remain a spinster. This caused derision in some elements of her society, including her wealthy neighbour Glynn Vivian, whom she regarded as crass and vulgar. It is clear from her diaries, however, that Amy Dillwyn did not on the whole regard spinsterhood as a terrible fate but looked forward to a future date when she could devote herself to charitable work within a religious order. Although this never came about, Amy certainly involved herself in charitable work, particularly in Killay, the setting of her novel, which was a village only about a mile away from Hendrefoilan House.

The upstanding inhabitants of contemporary Killay may well be shocked to find that in the mid nineteenth century their village was regarded as poor, rough, and dangerous. Many of the inhabitants were labourers who had come to

Swansea to work on the construction of the railway; a number were of Irish Catholic origin, and had large families. Amy, together with the local vicar's wife (who was also her aunt), took it upon herself to try to tame and educate these 'rough characters', partly by setting up a school there in 1858. Amy was not naturally inclined to teaching and she often found her duties less than congenial: 'There are 42 children in the school. I wish they weren't so dirty; they *will* clean their slates by spitting on them and the girls afterwards rub theirs with their pinafores, which are also used as pocket handkerchiefs. Now that's *nasty*. Then all their clothes smell so strong in hot weather one can hardly stand it, moving about from child to child and leaning over them, or else sitting in the middle of 10 or 12 standing close round one reading . . . Oh dear! I think trying to civilize Killay is very hard work . . .' (quoted in Painting, p.55) At other times, however, she does find some satisfaction from her work: 'One feels wonderfully maternal sitting surrounded by a class of the smallest trying to read.' (ibid.) A cold day, perhaps? Some of her comments on Killay convey a genuine frustration at the enormity of the task and her own inadequacy in trying to effect change: 'Why don't someone rise up with a vocation for Killay – I mean for doing what's wanted here. Someone is wanted to know Welsh and work hard and to know how to get hold of the people and keep the men from the public house . . . and someone to teach well. In fact a volunteer Welsh genius is required . . .' (ibid.) She was very active in helping the people of Killay in times of crisis, such as during outbreaks of cholera and typhoid, when she fearlessly visited and took provisions to the sick. Yet, as the early pages of *The Rebecca Rioter* show, she was quite able to mock her own 'Lady Bountiful' role and view it from the perspective of the poor.

Despite her charitable work, there is no doubt that Amy Dillwyn felt unfulfilled and vocationless from the mid 1860s onwards, as she frequently laments in her diary. She hated idleness and came increasingly to despise the triviality of the social world in which she moved. In the 1870s she began to be afflicted by an illness which, in her own words, obliged her to remain 'stuck to the sofa like a limpet on a rock' (*Painting*, p.71). It was during this period that she moved on from reading novels to writing them. She had just read and been hugely impressed by George Eliot's *Middlemarch*. After some failures and rejections, *The Rebecca Rioter* was published by Macmillan in 1880, its author's name being given as E. A. Dillwyn. Clearly, Amy did not want her work to be ranked among the burgeoning number of what George Eliot labelled 'silly novels by lady novelists' and therefore took refuge in the gender anonymity of her initials.

During the next decade, Amy wrote and published a further five novels. These tended to satirise the London life of the rich and leisured which she herself knew very well and to focus particularly on the social conventions restricting the possibilities of fufilment for women. During the 1880s Amy was also a regular, though anonymous, reviewer for the *Spectator* (whose editor was, conveniently, a friend of her father) which meant that she kept abreast of contemporary fiction and wrote perceptive reviews of major new work, by authors such as Robert Louis Stevenson and William Dean Howells. David Painting suggests that these 'literary' years of Amy Dillwyn's life were actually crucially important for her to crystallise and articulate her own feminist views, and proved a vital 'preparation for the actual challenges which were shortly to come her way and to change her whole life' (*Painting*, p.78).

In 1886 an event occurred in the Dillwyn family of sufficient melodrama to warrant inclusion in one of Amy's own later novels. Her younger sister, Essie, who had married thirteen years previously and was by then the mother of five children, abandoned her family and eloped to South Africa with an actor called Richard Pakenham whom Amy characterizes as 'a penniless scamp with a good voice'. In 1890 her brother Harry died, having contributed substantially to his own demise by his heavy drinking, and two years later her father also died, leaving Amy in the very precarious position of living in a house not her own, since Hendrefoilan House had passed to the next male heir, who was her nephew. Amy had lost her home but she had inherited the Llansamlet Spelter Works (a zinc factory) in her father's will; unfortunately, this turned out to be a loss-making enterprise which was currently £100,000 in the red. Instead of declaring bankruptcy and allowing the works to close, Amy took on the challenge to run it herself and to turn it around. 'I am becoming a man of business,' she wryly declares in her diary (Painting, p.85). This turn of events spelt the end of Amy's literary career but, in a sense, it is a continuation of the enterprise of challenge to paternal authority and patriarchal dominance.

After the humiliating auctioning of the entire contents of Hendrefoilan House in 1893, Amy moved out to modest lodgings in West Cross, where she lived a life of frugality and became widely regarded as an eccentric. However, her efforts to pay off all her father's debts and to turn around the fortunes of the Llansamlet Works were eventually successful. It was as if, released unexpectedly from the lap of luxury, she was able to find the vocation she had hitherto lacked. She became a recognizable, admired and formidable Swansea character though her fame spread much further afield. Despite her advancing years, she was hailed as one of the breed of 'new women' who were challenging the gender stereotypes of high Victorianism. 'One of the most original women of the age,' according to the *Pall Mall Gazette*, and it appears that Amy was not averse to playing up to the image. Having adopted a 'rational' form of dress which was regarded as excessively masculine, she compounded her transgression by taking to smoking large cigars in public. These traits, together with the enthusiasm with which she took up hockey and water polo in middle age, ensured that Amy would never be overlooked as an insignificant little spinster after the death of her protecting menfolk. Interestingly, she named her small house in West Cross 'Cadlys', being the Welsh word for a military camp: it was her miniature court (*llys*) in which she planned her battle (*cad*) against that male-dominated and socially divided world which had very nearly brought her to ruin.

During her later years, Amy played a prominent role in the public life of Swansea, using her enormous energy and managerial ability in the fields of education and public health. She was vocal in her support of the female dressmakers who in 1911 went on strike for better wages from their employer, the influential Swansea shopkeeper, Ben Evans. Unsurprisingly, she was also an ardent and hard-working supporter of women's suffrage, though she did not support violent methods in order to gain the movement's aims (as we plainly see in the authorial attitudes displayed in *The Rebecca Rioter*). By the time of her death in 1935, Amy was an independent woman of means and influence, disburdened of her industrialist's responsibilities by a judicious sale of the flourishing Llansamlet Works to a large German company.

The Rebecca Rioter is not a Welsh *Middlemarch*. It is, however, a fascinating example of the productive interaction between history and literature. If L. L. Dillwyn contributed to the telling of *his*tory, his daughter Amy Dillwyn moulds it to the telling of *hers*. Unlike her other novels, which have strong female protagonists, *The Rebecca Rioter* is an unusual novel for an avowed feminist to have written, adopting a male protagonist and a male voice. However, through her male mouthpiece and, indirectly, through the dominant figure of Rebecca herself in the novel, Dillwyn questions some of the cherished truths of her society and invites the reader to join her in that questioning and ultimately subversive attitude.

The Rebecca Riots

This manifestation of 'agrarian discontent', as the historian David Williams has termed it, began in South West Wales in the late 1830s. Country people, particularly farmers, rose up against what they saw as the oppressive and unjust imposition of steep taxes at the toll gates of rural Wales. The disguised Rebecca Rioters took their name and their text from the Book of Genesis, as Amy Dillwyn explains for her readers in a footnote to Chapter VIII: 'And they blessed Rebekah and said unto her . . . Let thy seed possess the gate of those which hate them.' This witty motto may also hint at the sense of dispossession of the largely Nonconformist common people in a state which had an established Anglican Church. In this context of religious division, Evan's surprise to learn from Gwenllian's Aunt Elizabeth that 'Church people used the same Bible as people did in chapel' (p.29) is quite understandable. A second upsurge of violence in late 1842 and 1843 moved from Pembrokeshire and Carmarthenshire to the Swansea Valley; the actual attack on the Pontardulais turnpike recounted in *The Rebecca Rioter* is a historically documented fact. That there was considerable popular sympathy for Rebecca and her followers is indicated by the fact that the rioters arrested at Pontardulais were not tried at Swansea, where a guilty verdict could not be guaranteed but had to be moved to Cardiff. David Williams, using L. L. Dillwyn's eye-witness account as one of his sources, informs us that the three men who stood trial, namely the ringleader, John Hughes (Jac Tŷ-Isha), along with David Jones, and John Hugh, were all sentenced to transportation, the former for twenty

years and the latter for seven years each. Amy Dillwyn's
fictional character Evan Williams, seems to be a composite
character, sharing some of the traits of all the accused.

Lewis Llewelyn Dillwyn's story

On the afternoon of Wednesday, September 6th, 1843, Lewis
Llewelyn Dillwyn was taking part in a cricket match on the
Crumlin Burrows when his bucolic pursuit was interrupted
by one Captain Napier, who brought news of an impending
attack by Rebecca Rioters on the Pontardulais Turnpike gate.
Having made plans to apprehend the 'mob', L. L. Dillwyn
Esq. calmly continued with his game of cricket.

Armed with 'a brace of large pistols . . . a brace of small
pistols . . . and a short heavy stick' (evidently taking no
chances) L. L. Dillwyn set out late that night with his companions and indeed came upon the children of Rebecca
attacking the said gate. 'We heard the sound of a great number
of horses, accompanied with blowing of horns, noises like
mewing of cats . . . and I heard a great noise, as of blows of
hatchets and other heavy implements, and the sound of
crashing of timber – I heard guns continually going off . . .'
Mr Dillwyn enthusiastically gets embroiled in the ensuing
fight, shooting a horse and whacking an attacker over the
head with a stake. The rioters are quickly routed and a handful
of the ringleaders arrested; Dillwyn returns home to Parkwern,
evidently satisfied with his night's work, at 'about five or
half past five in the morning.'

Amy's father's handwritten account of his personal
encounter with Rebecca extends over twelve small pages
which he dates September 10, 1843. As he declares near the
end of the narrative, 'I have now made these notes while
the whole of the transaction is fresh in my memory in case
at any future time I should be called upon to give evidence
of it.' The hand and mind of the careful magistrate is every-

where apparent in this less than gripping narrative. Although the events recounted are indeed momentous, L. L. Llewelyn succeeds in making them as unexciting as possible. A legalistic attention to detail robs the story of its drama and pace. At one point, for instance, a measurement of 150 yards is amended by a marginal note added and dated September 17 in which he informs the reader that, having paced out the distance, he finds that it is actually 100 yards. The latter half of the manuscript is noticeably written in less immaculate copperplate than the opening pages, as if to indicate the agitation of the writer as he actually recalls the fight. Also noteworthy are the many crossings-out and amendments which tend to occur at strategic points, as if the writer may have been attempting to protect someone or conceal an identity. There is, for example, a heavily deleted passage followed by a statement that he does not know who fired the shot. Clearly, the quasi-scientific observation and the detailed description of events, as if prepared for reading aloud in a court of law, have also been manipulated by the writer for his own ends. Because of the nature of the manuscript, we feel that we can almost *see* him doing it.

On the last page there is an additional paragraph in a different hand: smaller, rounder, more upright and distinctive than the other classic copperplate. It is signed E. A. Dillwyn and presents an update on what happened to the Rebecca rioters who were taken prisoner in the incident which her father has described. She also quotes the words of the Solicitor General who gave praise to Amy's father and uncle for 'manfully coming forward and risking their lives in the attempt to restore tranquillity.' In a sense, Amy's novel begins where her father's narrative ends, picking up on the consequences of his actions and focusing on the feelings and thoughts of the silent Other in L. L. Dillwyn's story: the Rebecca rioter himself.

ANALYSIS OF THE NOVEL

Evan Williams, the Rebecca Rioter

The narrative voice is one of the great successes of Dillwyn's novelistic method. From the start, Evan's first-person voice is established as distinctive: racy, lively, colloquial. It forms part of the characterization of Evan as an opinionated and forceful young man who is keen on questioning established 'truths'. Like his author, he is not afraid of depicting pillars of society, such as the landed gentry and the clergy, in a bad light. The picture he presents us of the Killay of his boyhood is realistic and believable, seen from the inside, as it were. Interspersed with his memories and his reflections on the contrast between then and now are his general reflections on class, morality, and reform. His view of the upper classes, their charity and their foibles, is satirical and absolutely irreverent. He has a keen eye for sham and hypocrisy and a strong communal feeling as well as a surprising capacity for tenderness, when he sympathises with the overworked horses pulling the gentry's carriage.

Evan is unpretentious and straightforward. He doesn't try to pretend to be a 'real hero' in his first encounter with Miss Gwenllian Tudor; he quite openly admits that he only stopped the runaway horses because he'd taken a fancy to Miss Tudor. His language is peppered with racy similes appropriate to his evening job as a poacher ('like a shot rabbit'). He himself is a hybrid character, as he explains, since he knows English as well as Welsh, having learnt it from his English mother. There is a picaresque dimension to Evan's character, too: he has a dry sense of humour and often lives on his wits. The scene in Chapter VI where he nonchalantly peels and eats a turnip (surely quite a tricky feat) while effortlessly outsmarting a policeman is a case in point.

Evan's character is, indeed, even more hybrid than he would have us believe. Many of his traits are borrowed from his creator so that there is a quasi-Shakespearean confusion of genders when Evan dresses up as Rebecca. If Evan is, in some respects, speaking for Amy Dillwyn, we are presented with a woman masquerading as a man who is masquerading as a woman. A bewildering performance indeed. In other senses, of course, Amy is speaking for the real equivalent of Evan, using her privileged class position to give a voice, albeit by a kind of ventriloquism, to the silenced Rebecca. There is an interesting and unexpected parallel between Gwenllian and Evan: both have Welsh fathers and English mothers.

Although Evan believes to a certain extent in the determining factors of heredity, environment, and gender, for instance, that men and boys *by nature* are hunters, and possess an instinct to catch and kill other creatures, at the same time, he also believes in the possibility and desirability of social *change*, otherwise he would never have become involved with Rebecca. Gwenllian too, believes in human perfectibility and, like her author, represents a younger generation willing to help effect that change. Perhaps the fact that both Evan and Gwenllian are singled out as hybrid characters, as mentioned above, makes them more open to the positive possibilities of difference, in contrast to the more rigid and monolithic attitudes of the older generation, represented by Squire Tudor and Aunt Elizabeth.

Evan's questioning of accepted morality is presented seriously, despite the fact that he himself is portrayed as something of an innocent abroad. Thus, his reflections on private property are quite cogent and pointed: how, he reasonably asks, can squires claim to 'own' wild rabbits? Later on, Evan makes generalised moral statements which do not appear to be questioned or denied anywhere in the narrative, such as: 'the life or death of a poor man . . . seems to make but very little difference in the world' (p.58) and 'the magistrates, to me and to most poor people, simply meant rich people who were in power, and who made laws to suit themselves, and then sent anyone who broke those laws to prison.' (p. 61) The novelist attempts to engage the reader actively in solving moral ambiguities and conundrums, particularly towards the end of the novel, where Evan as it were look out directly at us from the pages of the book and makes a direct appeal: 'was the fault wholly mine?' (p.173)

Class and Language

Evan has a strong sense of class solidarity as well as a sense of allegiance to a particular place, initially Upper Killay and later, Wales. Dillwyn depicts a society in which there is a mutual lack of respect among the classes. While Gwenllian Tudor's aunt represents a wholly unenlightened condescension towards the poor, whom she regards as being little better than animals (Chap IV, p.26), the latter display absolutely no deference towards their 'betters' – even the children of Killay take delight in commenting mockingly in Welsh about the aristocratic ladies. In Chapter II Evan indulges in a comic flight of fancy at the expense of the rich. He objects to his people being patronized by and lectured at by the charitable rich ladies who condescend to visit their cottages. What if the roles were reversed? The fantasy is brilliantly conceived and dramatized, in the present tense. Although the tone is comic, the underlying moral questioning is undoubtedly serious. Moreover, this concern with role reversal, exchange, and topsy-turveydom recurs in different forms throughout the novel. In a sense it both advocates reform of an antiquated hierarchical social system and at the same time displays the anxieties of those who stood to lose so much from that reform, namely Amy Dillwyn's own class.

Amy Dillwyn makes it clear that the language spoken by Evan and all of his companions is Welsh. In the direct speech there is an attempt to indicate this by a manipulation and defamiliarisation of the English language. Although contemporary readers might find this stylisation irritating, Dillwyn has clearly tried to indicate some of the actual features of the Welsh language in her 'translation'. Unlike Caradoc Evans, Dillwyn makes little attempt to mock or deliberately misrepresent Welsh speech. The most striking example of this experiment in tendering Welsh into English is the deformation of verb tenses: instead of the simple past tense, Dillwyn renders the typical imperfect tense of Welsh, literally ('I was want it . . .' (p.33) suggesting the normal Welsh phrase *'Roeddwn i eisiau ef'*). Moreover, she uses some Welsh words and translates some phrases and proverbs directly e.g. *heisht* (p.76 – hush); 'That is what do puzzle me clean' (p.118) (*Dyna beth roeddwn i'n methu'n lân â deall . . .*); 'Gwell angau na chywilydd' (p.65) ('Better death than disgrace.'); 'A *crot* of a boy' (p.34) (from Welsh *crwt* – boy). Thus, Evan is a representation of otherness in class and linguistic terms but it is an otherness which is deliberately mediated and softened for a potentially hostile readership. Arguably, Amy Dillwyn's evident sympathy with Evan may be conditioned not only by her liberal political beliefs but also by her feminism: the gender traditionally designated as Other, in Simone de Beauvoir's well-known terms, is as oppressed and neglected as the class and nation coded here as other.

Gender and Nationalism

Although we witness the men coming together as Rebeccaites and are even privy to their donning of female disguises,

Rebecca is consistently referred to in the novel in the singular and using the feminine pronoun, as if she were indeed a real person. It is clear that Rebecca is an emblem of roused nation-hood and, as in so many cases, the nation is gendered as feminine. During the episode in which Thomas Beynon makes his eloquent speech exhorting his listeners to action, there is a deliberate juxtaposition between the Queen and Rebecca. Beynon's listeners don't even know who the Queen is, and the message conveyed here is obviously that the Queen is not, in fact, the ruler of the Welsh. Instead, they construct for themselves an alternative ruler for their nation: Rebecca. A more vivid representation of the constructed nature of national identity it would be difficult to find. The maternal aspect of Rebecca's identity is underlined by the rebels' password: if challenged, they are 'going to their mother'. Rebecca is thus an emblem of the motherland and a feisty Maid Marian figure, 'sworn foe of injustice' (p.84). The male rebels are her 'children' (p.103). Dillwyn also manages to introduce a feminist note into the cross-dressing scenes: Evan discovers that women's clothing is extraordinarily uncomfortable and restrict-ive. Behind Evan's masculine complaints we can hear Amy Dillwyn, the exponent of 'rational dress'.

Structure and imagery

The novel is a framed narrative which has a prologue and epilogue ostensibly written by an editor camouflaged beneath the Eisteddfodic pseudonym, Morganwg. His or her identity is not fully revealed until the final page though we are informed immediately that Evan's rough 'Welshy' speech has been tidied up for our delectation. Clearly, this frame is a novelistic device designed to add a sense of authenticity to the account but it is also a tacit admission on the part of the novelist that this is a mediated narrative, mediated not in fact by 'Morganwg' but by his/her puppet-mistress, Amy Dillwyn herself.

There are undoubtedly devices in the novel which strike the reader as being clumsy or antiquated, particularly those features which are associated with the unrealistic genre of the romance. In a novel which is notable for its brisk realism, the device of the foundling Bill Jones turning out only too predictably to be Gwenllian Tudor's long-lost baby brother, Owen Tudor, strikes a jarringly far-fetched note. And yet this creaky device is important for Amy Dillwyn's political message. In common with other Victorian female novelists (notably Elizabeth Gaskell) Dillwyn sought to effect a reconciliation between what Disraeli called the two nations (the rich and the poor) through a redemptive and ultimately unrealistic rapprochement between the classes. At the end of the novel, with the old Squire representing the old, semi-feudal order, banished from the scene by the forces of Rebecca, the stage is set for a new order, presided over by the erstwhile Bill Jones, now Owen Tudor, who, having lived among the working classes, is naturally more sympathetic towards them. His name, combining echoes of Owen Glendower and the *mab darogan* Harry Tudor, suggests an optimistic look forward to a new Wales, unriven by class strife and with a vigorous sense of national pride. Possibly Owen may be seen as Amy Dillwyn's fictional representation of that impossible 'Welsh genius' who would come and lead Upper Killay out of its benighted state. Owen's green emerald locket, stolen twice over in the course of the novel before being finally returned to him, seems to be an emblem not only of his social status and familial identity but of his special election as a kind of saviour figure, a combination of rebel (Owen) and King (Tudor).

If the foundling device may be regarded as one of the least successful literary aspects of the novel, Amy Dillwyn's depiction of the landscape and the deployment of imagery may be counted among its primary strengths. The novel is a veritable litany of actual placenames from Swansea and its environs, while the flight of Evan and Tom over the Gower is plotted with topographical accuracy, from Clyne Wood to Three Cliffs Bay. Evan's narrative is full of *hiraeth* for the country he has left behind but, more than that, the suggestion is that nationalist feeling and pride is rooted in one's 'square mile', even if that happens to be the unprepossessing village of Upper Killay.

In addition to the hunting imagery which is so characteristic of Evan's speech and so apt, given his secondary occupation as a poacher, the novel is full of images associated with concealment and voyeurism. Evan is very much a watcher, from behind bushes, in ditches, hedges, caves, thatched roofs and castle walls. The connection with the novelist's observational role is clear, as is perhaps the inspiration Amy derived from her father's narrative, which speaks of creeping up on the rioters from a hiding place behind a hedge. At one point during the attempted escape of Evan and Tom, they find themselves on the castle walls of Penrice estate, actually looking down upon its aristocratic inhabitants and being able to spy on their activities. This is an apt physical representation of that topsy-turveydom about which Evan had fantasised in the novel's opening pages: what if the poor were to become the rulers, able to moralise and pass judgement on the actions of their masters? Like her contemporary, Thomas Carlyle, Dillwyn is contemplating here the potential dangers of 'shooting Niagara', the serious consequences of Reform.

Conclusion

Though Evan's belief in violent methods to solve social

problems is implicitly questioned in the narrative, there is no doubt that Evan himself is depicted in a positive light. Far from the primitive, animal-like creature Gwenllian's aunt would have us believe such a class of person would 'naturally' be, Evan is revealed as a thoughtful, passionate young man who takes moral issues seriously and who is possessed of a strong sense of loyalty and natural justice. Thus, Amy Dillwyn can be seen to be questioning the beliefs and attitudes of her own class, and indeed the actions of her own father. Moreover, in giving a psychological dimension to Evan's character which is shared by no other individual in the dramatis personae of the novel, Amy endows her protagonist with a complexity which belies his surface naivety. On two occasions in the novel, when he witnesses the attack upon the farmer John Smith on the moor (in Chapter V) and when he is hallucinating in his prison cell towards the end of the novel, we have a revelatory insight into the workings of Evan's mind which suggests not only the author's determination to transform this Other into a subject in his own right but also shows that Amy Dillwyn was a novelist of not inconsiderable skill and sensitivity.

Katie Gramich

References

Dillwyn Archive, University of Wales Swansea Library. Item 82: handwritten account by Lewis Llewelyn Dillwyn of his encounter with Rebecca Rioters at the Pontardulais Turnpike Gate, September 10, 1843.

David Painting, *Amy Dillwyn* (Cardiff: University of Wales Press, 1987).

David Williams, *The Rebecca Riots: A Study in Agrarian Discontent* (Cardiff: University of Wales Press, 1971).

Preface

The following autobiography was related to me by a man named Evan Williams. In transcribing it I have been obliged somewhat to alter the Welshy, and sometimes uncouth, language used by him, as otherwise it might not have been intelligible to the general reader. But in other respects the story is here presented to the public exactly as it was told to me.

MORGANWG.

CHAPTER I

Do not people's natures, more or less, take after the places where they are born and pass their lives? And is not a man much more likely to be rough and wild if he has been brought up in an exposed cottage whose walls rock and shake with every blast of wind, than he would have been if he had lived in some snug valley home, sheltered on all sides by hills and trees, and never had any further acquaintance with bad weather but what I may call an accidental one – that is to say, only knowing about it when he was out of doors – instead of being always in the midst of it, both indoors and out, and compelled to feel and know what it was like wherever he might be? If I am right in this idea, it will account for the Upper Killay folk being a rather rough set; for Upper Killay stands just at the edge of Fairwood moor, which is a place where you feel the whole force of every wind that blows, and where there always is some air stirring even though there may be none anywhere else, and where a hailstorm beats against you as if each stone wanted to make a hole through, and come out on the other side.

Properly to understand what the hail there could do, you should have seen the state in which the son of the minister at Three Crosses came home one day, with his face all over cuts and bruises, and one eye almost closed up.

Now the minister was a poor, weakly little fellow, who, though he never said a word against drinking, and was himself quite as ready for a glass as any of his flock, had yet a wonderful aversion to fighting, and was always preaching against it, and trying to put it down, declaring that whoever fought lowered himself to be no better than a beast. Of course he never allowed his children to do such a thing, so he was real mad when he saw his boy in this state, for he made sure he had been disobeying orders. The minister had had about as much liquor as he could carry that morning, and was not in the best of humours, and the boy would have had a most tremendous thrashing, only that he declared he hadn't lifted a finger against anyone – that it was nothing but the hail had knocked him about and made such a mess of him – that he and Jenkin Thomas had got caught in a storm as they were walking quietly over the moor – that one was as much hurt by the hailstones as the other – and that there was Jenkin Thomas in just the same plight to prove it. I remember that first made me notice how much worse the weather might be on Fairwood than anywhere else, for the hailstorms at other places that day had not been so remarkably heavy as far as I could hear. And I remember wondering, at the same time, why the minister should say fighting was so much worse than drinking, when, as far as I could see, a drunken man was a deal more lowered to be like a beast, than a man who had only had a quiet bit of a fight. But there! maybe a weakly little fellow like the minister never had the chance to find that out for himself – being sure to be beaten if ever he should try.

But, to go back to what I was saying, Upper Killay is so placed that it seems as if its inhabitants must naturally have more or less of a twist towards wildness; and when I was a boy, little or nothing was done to straighten this natural twist. People did not take so much trouble to improve one another in those days as they do now, and it seemed to be taken for granted that the state of life into which a man was born was as unalterable as his colour. If the parents were black, the children would never be white, and if the parents were uncivilised, so would the children be also to the end of their days, and it was no use trying to make them anything else.

Ideas have changed since then, and it has become the fashion to be very much interested in the education of the lower classes. There are folk now who make as much fuss about everyone's knowing how to read, and write, and spell, and understand poetry, geography, botany, history, and science, and such things, as if there could be neither health, strength, nor happiness without all this learning; and schools, churches, and chapels are springing up in all directions over the country. But in my time nobody had invented these new ideas, and the chapel at Three Crosses was the only 'civilising influence', as they call it, within reach of Killay. None of the children of the place knew what going to school meant, and, as a rule, we ran wild, and amused ourselves by getting into as much mischief as possible from morning to night.

Carriages were a great amusement to us children. Whenever we heard one coming we used to rush out and surround it; some running in front, some at each side, some clinging on behind, and all shrieking and whooping like mad. That is to say, we did this if we were not stopped; but the gentlefolks did not like it, and encouraged their coachmen to cut at us with their whips, so that we got to think that anyone who let us run after his carriage was sure not to be one of the real gentry. The people who suited us best were the Swansea tradespeople, when they went for a day's outing into Gower, and passed through Killay on their way there; for they used to throw us coppers to scramble for, and never minded how much paint we scratched off the vehicle they were in by hanging on to it – as indeed why should they, when it was a hired one and not their own? We generally liked to run as close as possible to the carriage, so as to look as if we were in danger from it (though in reality we were perfectly safe), for then, if there was any lady who wanted to be thought very feeling, she was sure to begin screaming and hiding her face, and exclaiming: 'Look at the wheel! It will go over the child – it will – I know it will! Oh, how horrid! I can't bear to look! Can't you stop the carriage? Oh, don't let the poor little darling be killed; do send it away!' and such-like nonsense, till her favourite young man comforted her, and threw us halfpence to get rid of us.

But with all their fine feelings none of these people ever took the trouble to get out and walk up the long steep Killay hill, so as to lighten the work of the poor animals that had to draw them; nor yet did they seem to see any cruelty in filling a big, heavy omnibus as full as it could cram, and making two half-fed, overworked horses drag it and them for some twenty or thirty miles on the hottest days of the year, and go at a trot for the best part of the way, whether it were up hill or down.

CHAPTER II

I was between fifteen and sixteen years old when first I fell
in with Miss Gwenllian Tudor, and the habit of mobbing
carriages – of which I have spoken – had a good deal to do
with that acquaintance. For though, of course, at that age it
was beneath my dignity to run after a carriage and hang on
to it myself; yet it was a different matter to watch the younger
children and help them with a shout or so if there seemed to
be a little extra noise wanted; and so there was nothing to
be wondered at in my throwing down my spade and rushing
off to the road, one day that I heard a sound of a voice calling
out, and of wheels and horses coming along quickly, as I was
working in the garden. On this particular occasion, however,
I soon saw that something had gone wrong with the coming
carriage. There was no one on the box, and the reins were
dragging on the ground; while the horses, apparently very
much astonished to feel themselves uncontrolled, and not
quite knowing what to make of it, were tossing their heads
and trotting along at a smart pace, though not actually running
away.

Inside the carriage were two ladies, one young and the
other elderly. The latter was in a desperate fright, and kept
screaming and trying to force open the door and throw herself
out; but the younger one, on the contrary, appeared quite
calm and composed, and was doing all she could to quiet her
companion.

They were coming from over Fairwood moor and going
towards Swansea, and were just beginning to descend the
first easy slopes of the long Killay hill. A little farther on they

would reach a much steeper part where the full weight of the
carriage would bear heavily on the horses and excite them;
and then kicking, and smashing the pole, an upset would
almost certainly follow. It was no business of mine, however,
and all I should have done would have been to run after the
carriage, when it had passed, so as to see what would
happen, if the young lady had not chanced to look quickly
round just as she got near enough for me to see her face
plainly.

For a moment her large dark brown eyes looked full into
mine, and seemed to be asking for help, and in that moment
a curious change came over me – I suddenly became very
pitiful for her, and anxious that she should not be hurt; and
so I sprang across the road to the side on which the reins
were dragging, and tried to catch hold of them as they swept
past me. I missed them and fell down, and very nearly rolled
under the wheels; but I was up again in an instant, and,
running down the hill at full speed, again got within reach,
and was able to make a second attempt. This time I was
successful; with the reins in my hand I ran beside the carriage,
pulling the horses back with all my might, and as they were
luckily not running away in earnest, they began to go slower
as soon as they felt a hand checking them, and had almost
come to a standstill when I struck my foot against a stone,
and rolled over the road like a shot rabbit. My hold on the
reins drew me towards the still-moving carriage, and, in trying
to keep my head away from the wheels, my right arm got
run over and broken. I heard the bone snap, and felt a shoot
of pain go through me, but I clung on to the reins with the
other hand all the same; so that the horses, still having my
weight dragging at the bit, pulled up a few yards farther on
in spite of my accident. By that time we were opposite The
White Swan public house, where two or three cartmen were
having a glass of beer. And after seeing one of them go towards

the horses' heads, and having the satisfaction of knowing that anyhow, as the young lady was now safe, I had done what I meant to do – which, to my mind, goes far to make up for whatever the doing of a thing may have cost one – I fainted away, and knew nothing of what happened for the next few minutes.

When I began to come to myself again I was lying by the roadside, away from the carriage, and the young lady was stooping down by me and wiping my face with a wet handkerchief; for my head had got slightly cut on the stones, and what with dust and blood together I was in such a mess that it was hard to tell what my hurts really were. I felt rather confused just at first, and lay quite still with my eyes shut, trying to recollect what had happened, and wondering how any human being could possibly touch one so gently; for her fingers passed over my face with no more weight than a summer's breeze, and I had never felt the like of their touch in all my life before. But as my mind got clear, and I remembered everything distinctly, I thought it was foolish to lie there like a log instead of doing anything to help myself; so I said in English (which I had learnt through my mother's being an Englishwoman): 'Will I do now, miss; or shall you be wanting to clean a bit more on me before I shall get up?'

'Do sit up if you can,' she replied, smiling; 'I'm very glad that you are not too much hurt to do it, as I was afraid you were.'

I *was* in a good deal of pain, there's no denying; but as I did not want her to think me a baby, to make a fuss about every little trifle, I sat up without any more ado, and looked about me.

The old lady had just managed to leave off screaming, and to get out of the carriage. She looked uncommonly scared at first, but when, after feeling and shaking herself all over, she discovered that no bones were broken, she became a little happier, and came up to where we were. Taking a great pair of glasses that hung round her neck, and spreading them across the bridge of her nose, she had a good stare at me, and then said to the young lady sharply:

'Really, Gwenllian, I am surprised at you! Leaving me to myself to get out of the carriage the best way I could, without anyone to lean on or to let down the steps for me, whilst you rushed off to attend to a boy whom no one ever saw before! I think you might have remembered that your father's sister has *some* claim to be considered before a mere stranger, and that there was no one but you to help me today, owing to our not having brought a footman with us. I only wish we had, and then this dreadful accident wouldn't have happened to us. But of course I know that Providence always settles everything for the best in some way or other, so I don't complain.'

Miss Gwenllian looked up pleasantly in the old lady's face, and answered: 'Well, aunt, I was coming to you in a minute if you had waited, only I couldn't help seeing to the boy who saved us first, for I wasn't sure but what he might have been killed, and I knew that you were all right.'

'All right, indeed!' exclaimed the aunt, indignantly. 'How can you suppose it possible to be all right after such danger, such a shock to the nerves? I believe I am very much hurt indeed, only I can't yet say exactly what the injury is, because I've not had time to ascertain. But after what I've just gone through I'm convinced that I'm shaken to a jelly, or bruised from head to foot, or something else quite as bad, I feel quite . . . quite . . . Ah, there! I can't call to mind the word for it at this moment, but it's something very unpleasant anyhow – a shivering, and a sort of an all-overishness – Ah well! young people have *no* consideration for old ones, and I daresay you don't care a bit for what I feel. To think that I, who am always so careful, should have had such a thing happen to me! Of course Providence always arranges everything for the best, and for my part, that *quite* satisfies me. But never again will I go out in the carriage without the footman.'

Just then the coachman came running up in a great state of mind. The accident had come about through his letting go of the reins to get off the box and knock a stone out of one of the horses' feet; for whilst he was picking up another stone for the purpose something had startled the animals and made them trot on suddenly before he could stop them. He now arrived where we were in a tremendous bustle – far too much taken up with thinking of the carriage and horses to pay any attention to the ladies. First he examined the horses, then the harness – prying into every strap and buckle to see that all was unbroken and in its place – then looked over the carriage to find out if a spoke of a wheel was cracked, a corner chipped or an atom of paint scratched anywhere – and then, when at last he had satisfied himself that no harm had been done, he drew a long breath, took off his hat, pulled out of it a great red-and-blue handkerchief with which he mopped his forehead, and exclaimed: 'Well, indeed to goodness, that is luck for me now! For what was I do, look you, if my carriage or my horses was take some harm to them? I think I was not able to look the Squire in the face again then. No, indeed!' He then seemed suddenly to remember the two ladies, and looked towards them. But, seeing them to be safe and sound, he took hold of the reins, climbed on to the box and sat there waiting for orders, and slowly getting over his flurry.

Meanwhile all the children of the place had come crowding round to us, and were behaving in a way that made me quite ashamed for them. Grown-up Welsh people are mostly better mannered than the English louts; and I was just getting old enough to be beginning to have some idea of politeness in me, so it made me cross to see the children fighting and

shoving for who should get nearest to us, and staring at us
as if we had been a show; and talking of the two ladies to
their faces and passing remarks on them just as if they had
not been there at all, or had had no ears to hear with. There
was not much chance of the ladies understanding what was
said, because it was all in Welsh; but I did not think of that
then, and was getting very angry with the children, and
wishing my broken arm would let me go and give them a
lesson in manners, when the young lady took my attention
off them by asking me my name.

'Evan Williams, miss,' said I.

'Do you live far off?' asked she.

'No, sure, Miss,' said I, "tis only just at the top of the hill
that we do live.'

'Well, Evan,' she said, 'if you think you are able to walk
now, suppose you and I go to your house together, for I want
to see you safe home and in someone's care before I go.'

Here, however, the old lady interfered.

'I really cannot consent to your doing anything of the kind,
Gwenllian!' cried she. 'Even if you don't mind what happens
to yourself, yet at all events you might have enough consideration for me, and for your dear father, and for the
servants, to keep you from rushing recklessly into any chance
poor person's cottage, where, for all you know, there may be
scarlet fever, or small pox, or measles, or whooping-cough,
or mumps, or any other of those diseases that people are sure
to bring home in their clothes from those sorts of places. As
I always say, Providence always settles everything for the
best; but that's no reason why one shouldn't take proper
precautions.'

But as Miss Gwenllian only laughed and shook her head
at all this, the old lady went on:

'Well if you *will* be rash and headstrong you *will*, and it's
no use my talking; but at least do ask the boy if he, or any

of his family are in charge of a medical man, or have been so lately.'

When I heard this I thought it was high time I said a word for myself. What a medical man might be I did not know, but what being in charge meant I did know, and thought that most likely 'medical man' was another name for a policeman. I felt injured at her being so ready to suspect us of getting into trouble, when I knew there was not a word to be said against one of us; and, if there had been, did she think it likely for me to go and let out about it to her, with the young lady listening, too? So I answered her sharp enough: 'Not a one of us do be in nobody's charge, nor haven't been neither not since three months back or more, when Squire Hughes's kipper was make some trouble with father about a couple of rabbits he was take home for someone else. But the meddlesome old kipper was not get nothing by it neither after all, for there wasn't nobody to prove nothing against father, and they had to let him go free directly. Indeed, and if that kipper was not mind what he was about I was not wonder if he was get more than he was like for himself some fine night – there now!'

When I finished speaking I saw that Miss Gwenllian was laughing, and this made me feel still more injured, for I thought she laughed because she did not believe me, and that seemed very hard when I had not told her one word of lies. For, whatever father might have done about the rabbits, at any rate it was quite true to say that no one could prove that he had come by them wrongfully. So, feeling, as I said before, very much offended I got up and began to walk away sulkily by myself, when Miss Gwenllian made matters all straight by saying that her aunt had only wanted to know if we had anyone ill at home. As to this I could give a thoroughly satisfactory answer (though what being ill had to do with being in charge I could not for the life of me make out); so then the aunt made no more objections, and we all three went up the hill to our cottage.

Mother was out just then, and we sat down and waited for her to come back, as Miss Gwenllian said she should like to see her before going away. The old lady filled in the time by asking me, in a very superior, condescending sort of way, how old I was, whether I went to school, what work I did, whether I was a good boy, and all kinds of other personal questions, such as most gentlefolks seem to think they have a right to ask when they go into a poor man's house. Sometimes, as I have listened to the things said by them in some cottage into which they have poked themselves without waiting to be asked or wished for, I have wondered how it would be if the poor man were to treat my lord's castle and its inhabitants in the same cool way. 'It's scarcely believable,' says my lady, tossing her chin in the air, 'and I never should have believed it if I hadn't heard it with my own ears! A man, a mere common man, walked into my boudoir without knocking, and asked me if my children were good at their lessons, and how my husband treated me, and whether I was saving, and had anything put by against bad times, and then said that the passages and stairs were not quite as clean as he liked to see them kept! I should like to know what business it was of his?'

'As for me, I very nearly fainted,' exclaims the eldest daughter. 'He asked me how old I was, and said he thought it his duty to speak to me about my clothes, to advise me to dress in a less expensive and more useful fashion, and to warn me against spending money on mere vain ornaments. A most impertinent scoundrel.'

'Impertinent scoundrel indeed!' echoes my lord; 'he actually told me that I was foolish to be running into debt, and said with a sigh that he was afraid I was too fond of the bottle, and had better check that in time, before the habit should grow too strong for me! I had him kicked out by the servants and ducked till he hadn't a dry thread about him; that's one comfort.'

'So I should think,' observes my lord's son and heir; 'the blackguard had the cheek to begin reading me a regular lecture, saying he hadn't seen me at church for some time, that young men should not neglect their religious duties, and that he wished me to read a tract against swearing!'

And then the whole family agree that if such inquis-tiveness, impertinence, and interference are to be tolerated the world may as well come to an end at once, and that the lower classes must be kept in their proper places and not allowed to trouble their heads about what does not concern them. Which means that what is – on the part of a rich man – called taking a kindly interest in his neighbours, becomes intolerable insolence on the part of a poor man, who is expected thankfully and humbly to welcome the visit of his superior at all times and seasons, and readily to answer whatever question may be put to him; even though it may have been asked and answered often before, and the questioner may be evidently talking as a mere matter of course, and without really bestowing either care or attention on the answer. Not that Miss Gwenllian was one of this sort, and she was always heartily welcome to whatever cottage she went; but then she was one in a thousand, and I never came across any other of the gentry who knew how to behave what I call properly to a poor person in his own home.

However, to go back to my story, there we sat waiting for mother to come back, with the old lady questioning, and giving good advice, and jabbering away at a great rate, till the behaviour of my little brother Bill rather hindered her, and kept her quiet. He and my sister Peggy with their fingers in their mouths (as is the way of children who are observing any strange thing intently), had followed us into the house from the road; and Bill, who had never seen any fine clothes before, was very much interested in a velvet jacket that the old lady was wearing. At first he only stared at it with all his eyes, but before long he drew nearer to it, and took to flopping his dirty hands on it, stroking it, and pulling gently at little bits of the soft stuff to see if it would come off. He was standing behind the old lady so that she could not see what was going on, and if ever she looked round his way, his fingers went back into his mouth like lightning, and he would be standing as still and innocent as possible while she looked at him. However, she seemed to be fidgety at his being behind her, and by-and-by she moved her chair right back against the wall so that he could not touch her without being seen. And then all of a sudden an idea came into his head. We had a kitten that he was mighty fond of, and thinking that it would be the same pleasure to the little cat to play with the funny new stuff that it was to him, he went and fetched her, and threw her right at the old lady's jacket without saying a word. Of course the poor kitten was desperately frightened. She just stuck her claws into the trimming for a moment, and then bolted upstairs mewing like mad, and very angry with Bill, and without doing any harm. But the old lady was as much put out as the kitten, and after jumping and screaming, stayed pretty quiet afterwards; though Peggy put an end to Billy's mischief by giving him a good smack on the head, and turning him out into the street to roar, or play with the other children, just as he pleased.

Soon after this mother came in, and Miss Gwenllian told her how I got hurt, and asked if she might send a doctor to me and might come back again herself to see how I was getting on. And then she and her aunt got into the carriage and drove off. I wanted to think of this new and wonderful young lady whom I had been listening to and looking at for the last hour, and I was sorry she was gone, so I would not speak to anyone else, and turned sulky to mother and Peggy, and sat silent in the corner by myself.

'Doctor indeed,' grumbled father when he came home and heard what had happened; 'and where shall she find a doctor as shall know so much as old Betty Perkins of Penclawdd? I do believe that a word from she and a look from her one eye shall do more to cure someone than all the doctors as was ever born, or all the oils as was ever mixed! Howsoever, if so be as the lady shall send a doctor I do suppose as she shall pay him too; so he can come if he do like, whatever.'

So the doctor was let to come and to attend to me, although the general opinion in the place was that it was a sin and a shame to let me be touched by a man who was paid the more the longer he kept me ill, and would be paid just the same if I died as if I got well; whereas old Betty Perkins never took a penny from anyone unless she cured him. Indeed I myself rather doubted whether my arm was having fair play in being put into the doctor's care; but, as Miss Gwenllian wished it, I made no objections, for she seemed to have bewitched me, and whatever she wished was my law. So I was pretty civil to the doctor for her sake, and generally did what he told me, unless it was anything that we all knew to be clean against reason – such as wanting the bedroom window to be kept constantly open. He was very fond about making a fuss about that; declaring that the air was thick and stuffy enough to breed a fever, and we used to save the trouble of an argument by letting him have his way unanswered and open the window as much as he liked whilst he was there, and then shutting it up tight again the moment he was gone. We weren't going to believe all the nonsense he talked, and have the whole family catch their death of colds with open windows as he would have liked us to do. Fresh, cold air is good for everyone in its proper place, but that place is not a bedroom. For why not sleep out of doors at once? And why have a bedroom at all, unless you want to avoid the outside air? As mother said, it was absurd to talk of letting in the cold outside air instead of the inside air which had been in the room since the night before, and the night before that, and for nights and nights before that again, making it warm and snug and comfortable! It was likely enough for a man who got more money the longer I was ill to want us to do such a silly thing; but it would be just as unlikely for us to be fools enough to do it – and no more we did.

CHAPTER III

Whether owing to the doctor's skill or not I do not know, but at all events my arm got well at last. As long as I was ill Miss Gwenllian used to come and see me constantly, sometimes reading to me, and sometimes bringing me wonderful jellies, and soups, and puddings, and creams, and such things, which were so good that I used to think they could not really be made from flour and eggs and meat, just like what we cooked for ourselves; or, if they were, how could they come to be so different and so much nicer? I remember one day when Peggy tasted some of my jelly, she said that if she had a cook who could make a thing like that, she should do nothing but go on eating it all day long, and I was pretty much of the same opinion myself.

Then the stories Miss Gwenllian read me were wonderful too. They were not all about good children who get rich and become lords and ladies, and bad children who come to a bad end; but they were stories of people who travelled about, and had adventures, and fought with lions, and bears, and wolves, and snakes; or else they were stories about fairies who could do whatever they liked with wands that they always carried in their hands – something like Moses's rod, I used to think.

All her stories were amusing, but on the whole the fairy stories were what I liked best of all, because the fairies were such strange creatures, you could never guess what they were likely to do next.

All this time I was getting more and more taken up with Miss Gwenllian herself, and I thought much more of her than of any one of the stories she told me. There was nothing that I would not do to try and please her, and whatever she told me to do I felt as if I certainly must do. I think it was her eyes that took hold of me more than anything else, and gave her the strange power that she had over me; and yet, though I felt how entirely she took possession of me and seemed to leave me no will of my own against hers, still that did not frighten me or make me want to stay away from her to keep myself free. On the contrary, the more I saw her the more I longed to see her.

Finding that I could not read or write, she began teaching me a bit; and when I was well she offered to go on with my lessons if I cared to come over to Penfawr – her father's house – to learn. I was only too glad to think that I should thus be able to go on seeing her, so it was settled for me to go to Penfawr every Sunday afternoon to be taught by her.

Penfawr was not very far from Swansea, and fully four miles from us. It was a large house standing in the middle of a fine estate which swarmed with game, for her father – Squire Tudor – was fond of his shooting, and preserved carefully, and thought a poacher the most wicked and hateful of mankind. I had never been there till the first Sunday afternoon after my arm was well. It was a beautiful day, and I did not reach Penfawr till later than I had meant to do, because I dawdled on the way to look at the sea – it looked so bright and blue from the top of Killay hill looking across to Swansea, and beyond that to Neath, and then Margam woods, and the Porthcawl sands, getting more and more blue in the distance, till nothing could be seen but one blue haze. And then again from the high ground near Hendrefoilan old farm there was Clyne wood lying green and red and brown close below me, and the Mumbles Bay beyond that, with little white-sailed vessels dotted about over the brilliantly blue water, and the coast of Devonshire on the other side, too far

off to show more of itself than just its lights and shadows –
it all looked so sunshiny and beautiful that it was no wonder
I stopped here and there to look at the view – a view, alas!
that my eyes will never see again in this life; though I often
think that, maybe when I am dead, my spirit will go back
and look at the dear old place which it gets sick and sore with
longing after.

Well, I got to Penfawr Lodge at last on that Sunday afternoon, and began to walk quietly up the drive without ever
dreaming what temptations were coming upon me. But the
Squire was a great preserver of game, and his grounds
abounded with rabbits, to say nothing of a very fair sprinkling
of pheasants as well; and the sight of the rabbits hopping in
and out of hedges and bushes on all sides, and the sound of
the crow and rush of pheasants rising in the plantations close
by were a sore trial to me; for it is the nature of most boys
and men – whether poor or rich – to want to catch and kill
any live creature whatever; and I longed greatly to have a
hunt after one or other of the furred or feathered animals that
seemed to make so little account of my presence. At first,
however, I resisted the temptation manfully; but presently I
could not help stopping to watch an old cock pheasant who
seemed to have hurt himself in some way, and to be unable
to fly. After looking at him, I could not keep myself from
going nearer to him – he ran away from me for a few steps
– I again followed him – he again ran on – and after repeating
this for two or three times I forgot all prudence and sprang
forward to catch hold of him, just managing to touch the end
of his longest tail feather. But I had been mistaken in thinking
he could not fly, for with one loud crow of alarm and disgust
he pulled himself free from me and flew off safely into the
cover – leaving me gaping like a fool with the feather in my
hand. His loud crowing frightened me; for supposing one of
those nasty prying keepers had been about, and had come

to the place and found me holding the feather? What a scrape I should have got into then! So I ran back to the road, and walked on quickly, resolved to take no more notice of any of these aggravating birds. But I forgot to harden myself against temptations from rabbits also; and when at last one silly young rabbit bounced out of the grass just under my feet, I did the thing that came natural to me without any consideration, and that was to throw my stick at him. It hit him hard, and he rolled over and over, and I pounced upon him to knock his brains out; but for as quick as I was, the troublesome little brute managed to give a loud screech first – which is a thing that I have noticed rabbits are very apt to do when one particularly wants them to be quiet. I popped him into my pocket in a minute, hoping no one had been in hearing; but by this time I had got to quite near the house, and before I had gone two steps farther, whom should I see coming towards me but Squire Tudor himself! I tried to look as innocent as possible; but the suddenness of the whole thing, and the knowledge of the rabbit in my pocket, made my heart beat fast, and I felt the blood rushing to my face and making me as red as a turkey cock. The Squire looked at me suspiciously.

'Did you hear a rabbit scream near here a minute ago?' asked he.

I had quite lost my wits, and I could only stammer, and hesitate, and say that I didn't know.

'Not know!' said he sharply. 'Don't tell me such nonsense. I can tell by the cut of you that you are no town boy not to know what a rabbit's scream is when you hear it, and you must have heard that one, as you aren't deaf. Why the rabbit can't have been twenty yards from where we stand. And I should like to know what business brings you prowling about my grounds with that great stick in your hand?'

I felt that I was getting redder and hotter than ever, and I could have beat myself for not being the same as usual; but somehow I could not think of the right thing to say, so, instead of telling him straight out that I was going to see Miss Gwenllian by her own wish, I only stammered out: 'Please, sir, I do always be having this stick when I do be out walking.'

'Humph!' growled he. 'And pray what may that be at the end of your stick? Give it here for me to look at.'

As he spoke I glanced at the stick, and in a crack at the end of it I saw, to my horror, a piece of the rabbit's fur stuck fast. I certainly do think that was the troublesomest rabbit anyone ever had the killing of: first to come thrusting himself in my way when I was not thinking of him, or wanting him; then, instead of being killed quietly, to go screaming out and bringing the Squire on me, and last of all to leave its fur in the stick to tell tales of me! I gave up the stick as told, and thought I would make a bolt and get off before more harm came; but this I was not let to do, for the Squire took hold of my collar at the same time he took hold of the stick, and held me fast while he examined the fur and made sure what it was.

'You young scoundrel!' he exclaimed, giving me a shake in his passion; 'I suppose next you'll tell me that you always have fresh rabbit's fur on your stick when you are out walking, and that you have leave to do what you please in my grounds! I can guess now how that rabbit came to scream. Give it up to me directly, for I warrant you've got it somewhere about you.'

Saying this, and without letting go of me, he rummaged through my pockets till he found the dead rabbit, which was still warm.

By that time he was in a towering rage.

'You impudent young rascal!' he cried. 'So this is how you spend your Sunday afternoon? Sauntering up my drive like a gentleman coming to call, and poaching my rabbits under my very nose! But I'll teach you to play such tricks here.'

With that he began trying to get the stick out of my hands to beat me with it, which I resisted vigorously; so there we were – struggling and fighting – he holding my collar with one hand, and trying to force the stick from me, and I holding on to it tightly and doing all I could to wrench myself clear from him, when Miss Gwenllian came upon us. We were near enough to the house for her to hear her father speaking angrily, and she had come out to see what was the matter.

'Oh papa, what is it?' she cried. 'Has that boy done anything wrong? He is Evan Williams, who stopped the carriage for us that day when the horses ran away on Fairwood, you know. He was to come and see me this afternoon, and I have been expecting him the last half hour, and wondering what had become of him.'

Till my young lady came out I had quite forgotten who I was fighting with; but when I saw her and remembered that the Squire was her father, I felt as ashamed of myself as could be, for what must she think to see me struggling with him like that? I left off fighting and stood quiet, and the Squire began to calm down also.

'Oh, so that's Evan Williams, is it?' said he, still keeping a tight hold of me. 'But I found the young scamp stealing my rabbits, on his way to see you. What does he mean by that? I'd have given him a rabbit and welcome, if he'd asked for it – aye, and a hundred of them, too – for the sake of his having saved you; but I vow he shan't help himself to them, and come poaching in my covers as he chooses, not if he'd saved you a dozen times over.'

Here I thought I would speak a word for myself, so I said:

'Well, indeed to goodness, and I was not mean to be stealing your rabbit, sir – no, sure! – but the thing was jump out at my feet so quick, look you, that I was knock it over before I was have time to think what I was do. And after all, you cannot say as I was steal it away, neither, for there it is for you, for sure'; and so saying I pointed to it lying dead on the ground.

'Ah! but how about it's not being stolen if I hadn't chanced to find you out?' said the Squire, with a half-smile coming over his face. 'I take it I shouldn't have ever seen much of that rabbit if I hadn't happened to be in the way, and to hear it scream some few minutes ago. However, attend to me now. I'll forgive you this time on condition that you promise never to poach here again, and not to let anyone else know that I ever did such an unprincipled thing as to let off a poacher caught red-handed.'

This I promised readily, and so ended my first meeting with the Squire. Would that it had been our last one too! But you see there seemed from the beginning to be a sort of fate that drew him and me into enmity, and made me quarrel with him almost in spite of myself.

I kept my promise about the poaching – because he was Miss Gwenllian's father – and never after touched fur or feather belonging to him. But all the same, I never can see that a man has any right to preserve hares and rabbits. When God made the land He put them into it just like the black-berries, and the mushrooms, and such like, for the good of everyone who lives there, and I cannot see what right any man has to take possession of them and call them his own. Why they are common property – just like any moor or common is common property on which the neighbours may turn out their horses, cows, geese, donkeys, pigs, and sheep to graze as they like, and which no man has a right to enclose and shut up from the rest. And don't the hares and rabbits belong to everyone in just the same way? And what right has a man to say they belong to him merely because they happen to be on his land? Therefore I never could see that it was stealing if a hare or rabbit happened to be on someone else's field when I took it, and no more did anyone else at

Killay call it stealing either – no – not even the minister. His flock paid him as much in food, or clothes, or work, or such things as they did in money; and if ever anyone brought him a pheasant or a partridge he made a fuss and did not like to take it, saying that he was afraid it had been stolen and that he did not like to receive stolen things. But with hares and rabbits it was quite different and he would take as many as were brought him without saying a word – which shows what he thought about the matter.

How odd it is that people should be so different in their ideas; for if any one had said such things to Squire Tudor I do suppose he would have broken the man's head, there and then.

CHAPTER IV

I have not yet told you whom Squire Tudor's family consisted of, but it is time I did so. He had no brother and only one sister – Miss Elizabeth. He had married an English lady, and had two children – a boy and a girl. The girl was my Miss Gwenllian, and the boy, Owen, was two years younger than her; but he had been lost in a very sad way when only a year old, which had been a terrible grief to all the family. All that was known about the matter was that one morning the child and nurse went out walking as usual, but were not come back at dinner-time. Mrs Tudor got uneasy, and was just going to send in search of them, when the nurse appeared without the child, wet through and crying bitterly. Her story was that she had been walking on the sands below Sketty, with little Master Owen in her arms, and had gone a long way out as the tide was lower than usual. She did not notice at first when the tide turned, and when she wanted to go back she found it was already running in between her and the land, so that she was quite surrounded by water. There was no one in sight to help her, she said, and she ran as fast as she could to where the water seemed most shallow, and began to wade through it, holding the baby as high as she could to keep him dry. The water was deeper than she thought to find it, and, as was a rough day and good-sized waves were running in, she had a hard job to keep her feet. At about the middle of the passage she stumbled over a stone and fell down. Just at that moment a big wave had come and washed the child out of her arms. She had had the greatest difficulty in getting safely to land herself, and she had never managed to get hold of the child again, so he had been carried out to sea and drowned.

This was the nurse's account of the matter, and she seemed almost out of her wits with grief; and no one could possibly blame her for her carelessness more than she blamed herself. It was thought certain that the body of the child would be washed ashore somewhere, and for days and days the Squire had people searching for it all along the coast between the Mumbles and Swansea. But it was no use. Some strange current must have carried the body away, for nothing was ever seen of it, nor yet of the little cap, and hood, and ribbons that the child wore.

Poor Mrs Tudor, who had never been very strong, could not get over the shock of the child's loss, and pined away more and more, till at last she died when Miss Gwenllian was about eight years old. And ever since that, the Squire's sister Miss Elizabeth (not being married) had lived with him and taken charge of the house for him.

Miss Elizabeth was a well-meaning old lady, I do believe, but she had queer ideas in many ways, and I never got to be very fond of her, nor did she ever take to me at all – which perhaps may have had something to do with it. She never seemed to think that poor people could be quite the same flesh and blood as herself. If they were sick, or in want, she would very likely try to be kind to them in her own fashion; but then it was in a grand, high sort of way, more as if it was a dog or cat that she was caring for than a fellow-creature, who could think, and speak, and feel, and have a soul just like one of the gentry.

One curious thing about her was that she was always making plans to keep out of every possible accident and misfortune, and yet always finished up with her favourite remark that no doubt Providence always settled everything for the best. As she said it so often, I suppose she really believed it, but she certainly seemed to think she could help in the arrangement of things a good deal herself. She had the greatest possible dislike to Dissenters, and seemed to think it almost wrong to speak of them – just as if the very word might take root in the ground and spring up as an enemy ready to fight against the Church. I am sure she was very doubtful if any Dissenter could possibly be saved – and if so, no doubt there was some reason in her horror for them.

Poor Miss Elizabeth! I well remember one Sunday that Miss Gwenllian was ill, she asked her aunt to teach me instead of her – and a funny lesson it was. To tell you the truth, I did not like the change at all, for I was not much set on learning unless it was from Miss Gwenllian; but as I did not want to vex her by not doing what she had settled for me, I set to work with Miss Elizabeth, who had never before taught any poor people except a class of nice tidy little Church children at the Church Sunday school near Penfawr, and to whom I and my ignorance of what she thought I ought to know, were about as much of a shock as a bucket of cold water thrown over her would have been.

She began by asking me questions out of the Church catechism, thinking that of course I must know that. When she found I could not answer – as how could I, when I knew nothing whatever about it, and she held the book so that I could not see into it over her shoulder and read the answers that way? – she got cross, and gave it to me to learn, saying that she was sure that I was only pretending not to know, that I could answer well enough if I chose, and that I was to sit quiet and learn the first page by heart.

I was always pretty quick at learning things, so I soon knew my lesson, and when she had heard me say it without a fault, she began to look rather pleasanter.

'Now I shall see if you understand what you have learnt,' said she. 'What place were you taken to when you were baptized?'

'Nowhere, mum,' answered I, not guessing what answer she wanted.

'Oh, were you baptized in your own home, then?' she asked.

'No, sure,' replied I, not quite understanding what was the good of all questions; 'I was not baptized never – not nowhere at all.'

She did look shocked at this, and I saw that she gave a sort of shudder, and seemed to draw away farther from me as if I had been a toad, or snake, or some poisonous creature.

'Never baptized at all!' she exclaimed. 'Oh dear! How can Gwenllian be so foolish as to have to do with a heathen like that! Never baptized! And says he doesn't know the catechism! Who would have thought it possible that a niece of mine should take any interest in such a boy as that, and have him for her pupil?'

And she looked so horrified, and went on exclaiming 'Oh dear!' and 'Is it possible?' till I almost began to think I really must be something very dreadful without knowing it. Then she seemed suddenly to make up her mind that she was going to make me good all at once by talking, so she fell to preaching at me. Such a preaching as it was! I tried to listen at first, though I did not understand it at all; but, after a bit, the steady hard sound of her voice going on and on without changing made me drowsy, and I fell fast asleep. From this she woke me with a box on the ear, declaring that it was no use trying to mend such a bad boy as I was, and that she would have no more to do with me. And from that time forth she never tried to teach me anything again.

The footman at Penfawr, with whom I was rather friends, told me that after that Sunday she told Miss Gwenllian she really ought to have nothing to do with me; but that Miss Gwenllian only seemed amused at her aunt's being so shocked, and said that the worse I was the more reason there was to try and teach me something better.

Another thing I heard from my friend the footman was that, when my arm was broken, the Squire had not at first been very pleased at Miss Gwenllian's going to see me, saying that the people at Upper Killay were a bad, rough lot, and that he did not want to have a daughter of his going amongst them, considering what awkward stories were told sometimes about what happened to the Gower farmers on market-days. Report said that when farmers from Gower were going home with the money for whatever they might have sold in Swansea, if they were the worse for liquor, as they were very apt to be – being sometimes so drunk that they had to trust entirely to their horses to get them safe home – it was an even chance but what some of the Killay or Upper Killay people managed to rob them as they crossed Fairwood moor, and that many a farmer who had money when he left Swansea had none by the time he got back to his farm in Gower. And so it was partly from this that we came to have a bad name at Upper Killay, though the stories had never been proved against us. However, Miss Gwenllian got over her father's objections – she never being afraid of anything for herself – and got leave to do as she pleased about coming to see me, and having me at Penfawr as well.

She got to make a pretty tidy scholar of me before long, for – like most Welsh people – I was quick to learn when I had a mind to it; and I had mind enough to learn when I saw how it pleased her. She taught me not only reading and writing, but something about religion as well, and I was surprised to find that Church people used the same Bible as people did in chapel. But I do not know that my religious teaching got very far. I was quite satisfied that whatever she taught me must be all right, and I wanted to think and do whatever she wanted me to think and do; but I believe that if she had tried to teach me wickedness instead of goodness it would have been all the same to me, and I should have been just as willing to learn

it to please her. Only I suppose that is imagining an imposs-
ibility, for if she had been wicked she would have been quite
different from what she was, and if she had been different
from what she was, then she could not have had such a
strange attraction for me.

If she had known how I believed in her she might have
saved herself a good deal of time and trouble in trying to
make me understand why one thing was right and the other
wrong, for if she had merely said 'This is right,' and 'That is
wrong,' I was quite ready to take her word for it without any
reasons. I do not know if she believed the stories about the
Gower farmers or not, but she certainly took a good deal of
pains to impress upon me the wickedness of stealing. Possibly
she may have had some idea of the temptation to rob a rich
farmer coming in my way some day, and wished to guard me
against giving way to it. But if so, it would have been much
simpler to tell me straight out that it would displease her if
I were to do such a thing, for that would have been quite
reason enough to keep me from doing it.

I was very happy then, going to see her and learn from her
weekly, and I should have liked it to go on for ever. But it
came to an end about two years after first I had known her
– when I was just seventeen – for she and her father and aunt
had to go and travel in foreign parts on account of her aunt's
health, and Penfawr was to be shut up for some time –
perhaps for two or three years.

CHAPTER V

No account of Upper Killay would be complete that said nothing about Philip Jenkins, the landlord of The White Swan, which was the only public-house in the place. A big strong man was Phil, who never looked anyone straight in the face, but mostly kept his eyes on the ground, and slouched about with a hang-dog sort of look. He, and his wife, and his daughter Jane lived alone in the public-house, keeping no servant, and doing the work of it themselves; but poor Jane was not good for very much, being half-witted from a fall she had when a child, and a good deal crippled with rheumatic fever besides. Almost everyone was sorry for the poor half-starved girl, except her father, who always seemed cross with her for being so helpless and sickly, and who sometimes ill-treated her shamefully when he was drunk.

It was not very often that he did get drunk, but now and then he would go on drinking beer steadily for a week or fortnight, till he was no better than a madman. I remember once when he had got himself into this state, he took a candle and went upstairs to where his wife was in bed and set her cap on fire, and she had to jump up, and tear off the cap, and run out of the house for her life, with him following her with the candle. He only did it to amuse himself, as he had no quarrel at all with her! Another night, when he was in one of his drunken fits, he turned his wife and daughter out into the snow, and they would have had to sleep under a hedge if one of the neighbours had not taken them in. And another time, again, I remember we were in bed asleep, when we were woke by a knocking at the door, and there was poor Jane

Jenkins with bare feet and nothing on her but her nightdress, and with blood streaming down her face, standing outside in the bitter cold, almost out of her wits with fright, and begging us to hide her from her father. He had gone and pulled her out of bed, and begun beating her, and would have killed her very likely, only that her mother had managed to get the door open for her to escape.

The only person who had much chance of managing him when he got very violent was his son Jim. More than once I have known Jim being fetched from his work to keep his father in order, and then Jim would go and give him a good clouting, which would bring him to his senses for a bit.

This sketch of the landlord of our public-house will help you to understand what we ourselves were like. For no one would suppose that the men who were on friendly terms with Phil Jenkins, and drinking nightly at his tap, could be anything but a rough set of fellows. And now that I have told you this, I will go on with my story.

Early one Saturday morning after the Tudors had gone abroad, I was standing in the road near our cottage, when a man on a gray horse came trotting along towards Swansea, leading another horse by the halter. I knew the man by sight as he generally went past on market-days, and knew that he was one John Smith, who had a farm at Rhossilly – far away down in Gower. He was a sulky, close-fisted, cross-tempered fellow – always ready with an oath and a cut of his whip for any child or animal that come in his reach – and seldom known to go back from market thoroughly sober; drink being the only kind of extravagance of which he was ever guilty. Tom Davies – son of old Joe Davies who lived nearly opposite to us – was just then lounging in their garden with his back to the road so that he could not see who went by, and I heard him say to Rees Hughes, who was in the garden with him and looking over the hedge, 'What be all them horses, Rees?'

'There do be only two,' replied Rees. 'It do be John Smith riding into market, and was take 'nother horse with him – take it to sell, I do suppose.'

'Why what can a chap like he want with money, I wonder?' said Tom laughing. 'What pleasure was it be to he to have more than he do want for his drink? For he was never spend a sixpence on nothing else in all his life, I do believe. Now if he was give the price of his horse to me that was be something like, now, and then I was buy something nice for pretty Martha Williams over the way.'

For Tom was very sweet on my eldest sister, Martha, and was always making eyes at her, and wanting her to walk out with him on Sunday afternoons, and to take him as her young man. Whenever he could get a little money he was sure to make her a present of some kind; but that was not often, for he was so idle that he barely earned enough to wipe off his score at the public when he could get no more liquor on credit, and to pay his father for boarding and lodging him. His attentions to Martha met with hardly any encouragement, and yet I sometimes fancied she had a sort of liking for him in the bottom of her heart, though she did not show it.

'Well,' said Rees Hughes, speaking in a joking careless way, but watching Tom closely to see how he would take the notion, 'a person was not have much trouble to take his money from Smith if he do be so drunk going home tonight as he was last Saturday. Suppose if us was to take it, and go halves in it, Tom? I do want some money, as well as you, for a wonder.'

'Well, indeed, and I do think the wonder shall be when you was *not* want it,' replied Tom, laughing; as well he might, for Rees drank away every farthing as soon as he got it, and was generally trying to borrow from someone. 'But I was want it the most, you see, for to get something real pretty for Martha Williams.'

Here I interrupted them by saying: 'Is it for Martha you
shall get it, Tom, or for the cat? The last time you was bring
a ribbon to Martha you know she was give it to Bill for his cat
before ever you was out of the house.'

I could not resist the chance of teasing Tom by putting him
in mind of this, though I was half afraid of chaffing him, too,
as he was four or five years older than me, and could lick
me easily. Both he and Rees started when I spoke, for neither
of them had known that I was near them. Tom coloured as
red as fire. Coming close to the hedge he shook his fist at me,
saying: 'Just you keep yourself to yourself, and mind your
own business, you young Evan. If so be you was not brother
to Martha I was give you a thrashing for your impudence
now d'rectly minute. I was not want to ask you leave before
I was make a present, and you was not know nothing about
how girls do take presents from their young men neither. A
crot of a boy like you!'

After that I went off to work, and heard no more of what
passed between Rees and Tom, nor did I think of their conversation nor of them again that day, except that I wondered
why Martha did not seem more willing to have Tom. For
he was a tall good-looking young fellow, and good-natured,
in spite of his idleness; he was the sort of man who was likely
to be kind to his wife, and not to beat her – as was a common
custom with the husbands about Killay and Three Crosses.
Now if it had been Rees Hughes that was courting her it
would have been quite another matter, for he was sulky,
gloomy, and disagreeable at the best of times. You could put
him in a passion in a minute, and when he was angry it was
always a word and a blow with him – and the blow was sure
to come first. He was so often out of temper that he hardly
had time to get good-tempered between whiles, and when he
was cross I used to think that he would have kicked every
live thing he met if he had dared.

Well, on the evening of the Saturday I am telling you about, I had to go down to The White Swan to fetch a drop of gin for father, who mostly had his liquor at home on market-nights, because he did not like the lot of strangers coming clattering in at the public. He was fond of giving his opinion on things in general over his glass and his pipe; and hated to be hurried, and put about, and interrupted when speaking. He liked to speak slow, and to stop to take breath pretty often, and then go on again with what he was saying, and have it listened to in peace and comfort; and of course this was impossible when there were noisy market people scuffling in, and wanting their beer and spirits all in a hurry, and then bustling out again. So on Saturday nights father seldom went down to the public, but had his drop of gin and smoked his pipe quietly at home.

When I got to The White Swan it was full of business, and I had to wait some time for other customers to be served before I could be attended to. Whilst I was waiting, John Smith came in, far gone in liquor already, and calling for hot brandy-and-water to warm him before he rode across 'that cursed cold moor,' as he called Fairwood. He was tipsy enough to be talkative, and went on bragging about the horse he had sold that day, and about how sharp he was in getting a good price for whatever he sold; and he dropped hints, too, about something he had that day had given him for his wife, which he was sure must be uncommonly precious considering the fuss that had been made over it by the party who had handed it over to him.

There was another Gower farmer in company with him who was very fairly sober, and who did what he could to keep Smith quiet and to get him to come away in reasonable time. But it was no use – Smith would not pay the least attention to him – so at last he went off by himself and left Smith to get as much more drunk as he pleased. When I had got what I was sent for and went back to our house, he was still there drinking and boasting that such a man as he would soon make his fortune – what with his own cleverness and the luck of people sending treasures to his wife in a strange and mysterious manner.

Nearly an hour later than this, mother suddenly remembered that she wanted our donkey brought in that night, and as it was out grazing on Fairwood as usual, she sent me to fetch it home for her.

It was too dark to tell one donkey from another by that time; but our donkey knew me well, and would run to me like a dog, and the moon was rising besides, and would soon be giving plenty of light; so there would be very little difficulty about the matter, and I just put on my cap and went to the edge of the moor, where the donkey's usual feeding-place was. No donkey was there, however, which was provoking; for Fairwood is a good large space of ground to have to hunt over for an animal; and besides, it is full of bogs which the moon was not yet giving light enough to enable me to avoid.

I thought the most likely place for me to find the donkey was at a spot where I knew there was some very good grass, a few hundred yards beyond the first sign-post that stands on the Swansea side of the moor; so towards that I walked, keeping along the grass by the edge of the road instead of taking the shortest cut, because I did not want to get into the bogs.

Just after I had passed the sign-post I heard a horse's feet coming along on the road, and stood still to watch it go by. There was only light enough for me to make out that it was a gray horse and that its rider was either very ill or very drunk, for he was almost bent double in the saddle, now and then trying to sit upright and failing to do so, and swaying about from side to side as if any jolt or stumble must topple him over. It was quite plain that the horse was taking care of the man, instead of the man minding the horse.

I thought the horse looked a good deal like the one Smith had been riding that morning, and the man looked like Smith himself; but it was too dark for me to see them clearly.

The horse seemed to know how helpless its master was and was going very quietly, and they had gone about thirty or forty yards beyond me, when I suddenly saw the dark figures of two men appear by the roadside from behind a mound that had kept them hidden till then. Some high furze bushes were between us which prevented their seeing me in the uncertain light; but by moving a little and peering through the bushes I could make them out and see what they did.

One man caught the horse's bridle and stopped him, while the other pulled the rider on to the ground and began turning out his pockets. I was so taken by surprise, and it all happened so quickly, that at first I quite thought I must be dreaming; but no, I rubbed my eyes and looked again, and no doubt there was someone being ill-treated close to me – a robbery was going on under my very nose!

If you think that I was very much shocked when I realised this, you are quite mistaken. At Upper Killay, where I had lived all my life, ideas of right and wrong were rather mixed, and people generally thought that might was right; and what was the wonder of that, when no one had ever taught them any better? Therefore it did not seem very dreadful to me that two men should help themselves out of the pockets of another man who had been fool enough to get into such a state as not to be able to take care of himself. Indeed, as soon as I got over my first surprise, I thought I would like to go on and get the men to let me have a good gallop on the horse before its owner would be wanting it again – for I dearly loved riding – when Miss Gwenllian and her teaching suddenly came across my mind and made me stop. Would it not vex her for me to be mixed up in any way with a robbery? No doubt she would most likely never hear anything about the matter. But I felt as if it would be unfaithful to her to do a thing – because she would not know it – which I should not do if she did know it. That is not the way to treat a person one really cares for. If she were with me at that moment, what would she have me do? I wondered. Would she think I ought to try and stop the robbery? But she would surely not want me to do what was impossible; and it clearly was impossible for a lad like me to stop two full-grown men in what they chose to do. Besides, though I had been taught not to steal myself, yet I had not been taught that I was bound to interfere with another man's stealing; so I resolved to keep out of sight and not meddle in the matter. Accordingly I squatted down behind the furze and watched what happened.

The two men had pulled out the rider's purse, and in moving him about they had let his head roll into a little stream of water, and I suppose the fresh cold wetness brought him a little to his senses and partly woke him up from the stupid state of drunkenness in which he had hitherto been. He gasped and looked around him, and suddenly pressed his hands tight over one place in his coat, as if there was something particularly valuable there; and then he rolled his head slowly towards the man nearest him and had a good stare at him. Next I hear him drawl out in a dull stupid sort of way:

'Just you let me alone, you villain; never fear but what I'll pay you out for it else, as sure as my name is John Smith.'

It was a foolish thing for him to say; for though at that time he was not sober enough to be likely to remember the face he looked at, yet the robber either did not think of that or else would not trust to the chance of it. With a fierce oath he swore that Smith should not know him again and, as he spoke, he struck Smith two or three tremendous blows on the head with a heavy stick that was under his arm; the thud of the wood crashing on the skull reached my ears quite plainly and made me shiver. This was getting more serious than a mere robbery, and I felt rather frightened. When the robber spoke, his voice told me what I had suspected before from his appearance, and that was that he was Rees Hughes. And now the other man, who was holding the horse, spoke also, and I recognised him to be Martha's admirer, Tom Davies!

'Stop now!' exclaimed he in a frightened voice; 'you do have killed the man for sure, and whatever was us do now? Was you not promise me faithful as no harm shall be done to him, before ever I was willing to go with you?'

Hughes leant over the man, and felt if his heart was beating.

'I was not think he dead neither,' answered he, after a pause; 'but, and if he were, it is better so than for he to be alive and swearing to us at the next sessions. And us have got his money whatever.'

'Well, us have got what us did want then, so there shall be no more use to stay here longer,' said Tom, looking nervously round; 'be quick, man, do, and come you away before someone shall come now.'

'Take you the saddle and bridle off the horse first,' returned Hughes; 'it will be pity to let them go when us do have the chance of them. And stop you while I do see if he have a watch about him too, for, when a bit of luck do come in our way, us may so well as not make the most of it.'

While Tom ungirthed the saddle, and slipped off the bridle, Hughes poked and fumbled all over Smith's body, and, taking out his knife, ripped open that part of the coat which Smith had tried to cover with his hands, and pulled out thence something that looked to me like a book, or box, or parcel. It now crossed my mind what I had heard Smith saying that evening at The White Swan about some precious thing he was taking to his wife. I also recollected that Rees Hughes had been in the public at the time, though Tom Davies had not; and I guessed what Hughes had just cut out of Smith's coat must be the very treasure itself. Hughes turned his head quickly towards Tom to see if he were noticing him. But Tom was on the other side of the horse, and busy about the saddle, so Hughes said nothing about the parcel, but hastily pocketed it, and pretended to have found nothing more, and grumbled at Smith for not wearing a watch. The horse would not have been safe to keep, so it was turned loose on the moor as soon as the saddle and bridle were off, and then the two men gave a last look at their victim, who still lay on the ground without moving.

'I do think in my heart he was dead,' said Tom uneasily, 'and maybe they shall find us out, and us shall get hanged. And yet I can swear as I was not lay a finger on him, and so can you say the same too for me if you shall choose. You know it was you did it and not me.'

Hughes laughed roughly. 'But perhaps as I shall *not* choose,' replied he, 'and what was become of you then? Why shall someone believe your word more than mine, if I was swear as it was you struck Smith, and that I was try to hinder you? But don't you be a fool to frighten yourself like this. Us shall hide away the saddle and bridle somewhere till all's forgotten, and there shall not be a soul as shall suspect us in the matter. Why shall someone think of us more than anyone else, when none of Smith's things shall be found with us?'

'Was not we say something about it this morning when Evan Williams was by?' said Tom suddenly.

'Well indeed and I was forget that,' exclaimed Hughes with an oath, 'but 'tis true for you too. If he was to say a word now – but if he does it shall be the worse for him! 'Tis not likely though, as someone shall ask him about Smith, and he shall not want to go talking of it of himself – why should he? And maybe as he was not hear what we was say neither – with his head always full of that young lady he is crazed after. Well – come you now, for it is time to get away from here.'

Then they went away over the moor together, passing near enough to me to make me in a fright lest they should see me. For I had always been half afraid of Rees Hughes since I was a boy, and what I had just seen and heard did not make me feel any more confident than before in him. So I never moved from my place till they were well out of sight, and then I stood up and wondered what to do next.

Was Smith dead, or was he not? I was afraid to go up to him and make sure as he lay there like a log. If he really were dead, I almost thought it would be better not to know it, for it seemed to me so dreadful to be all alone with a dead man on the wild moor – and at night too! For an instant I had a mind to run after Hughes and Tom, thinking I would rather have any company than be left alone with the dead. But then perhaps he was not dead after all – and if I joined the other two men, perhaps Hughes might think I knew too much, and do to me as he had done to Smith – so I gave up that idea.

I looked at the body again. It was horribly quiet. The face showed ghastly white in the light of the moon, which had now risen and shone brightly; and nothing stirred about the head except some locks of hair which were lifted by the wind and blown carelessly to and fro. Close beside the head was a dark, shining, narrow line, that moved slowly across the road, and that I thought must be blood. Then I believed the man was certainly dead.

I had never seen a dead person, and I now felt terribly afraid of death. It was so awful for a living, breathing, reasoning creature, just like myself, to be suddenly changed into a mere lump of earth – and yet a lump of earth that *looked* exactly like a man. And then this horrible change must have come over what I was watching even while I was watching it! How could it be? There was a Something in the man that made him live – and how could that Something go out of him without my seeing It go – and I so close by?

That Something must be somewhere else now that It had left
the man. It could not be far off, for surely It would want to
stay – if only for a short time – yet at least long enough to
see what became of the body in which It had lived. Where
was It? It must be very near to me. Perhaps It would take
some fearful shape – perhaps It was close behind me at that
moment – perhaps It was so near me that if I moved I should
touch It! The mere idea of such a thing made me shudder
and tremble. I longed to make sure whether It were behind
me or not – but I dared not look round to see – for if It *were*
there, whatever should I do? And how should I bear the sight?
I was quite miserable. I dared not move, and yet I dreaded
staying where I was – and all the while my eyes were fixed
on the shining dark pool that kept increasing and creeping
over the road by the side of the head – and the wind went
on tossing about the hair over the terribly quiet white face
that lay there looking so like a man – and yet, perhaps, not
a man! Nothing else moved; nor did I. The terror of what I
might see or touch if I changed my place, kept me as still as
the body in the road; and there we stayed in the moonlight
like two corpses – one lying down and the other upright –
for some time, but how long it was I do not know.

At last a very feeble groan came from the horrible thing
that I was looking at – and immediately it was no longer
horrible to me. If it could groan, it must still be a man – and
the Something I had feared must be in Its proper place, and
not lurking behind me, or on either side of me, or in any
unexpected situation – so I took heart again and went up to
Smith. I raised his head off the ground – not knowing what
better to do for him – and as I did so, his eyelids slowly
opened. The eyes, however, did not look as if they knew
anything, and after staring stupidly up at the sky for a minute,
they closed again. I was a good deal puzzled what to do now.

I did not want either to go and fetch anyone else, nor yet

to be found there alone with Smith; for I thought I should have some trouble in proving that it was not I who had knocked him off his horse and robbed him, unless I cleared myself by telling of Rees Hughes and Tom Davies, and that I certainly did not want to do. For one thing, it would be quite against the Killay ideas of morality to bring two neighbours into trouble; and, besides that, I was fond of Tom, and was a good bit afraid of what Hughes might do to me if I were to anger him.

Yet I did not like to go away and leave poor Smith altogether alone – however little use I might be to him by staying – and I was fairly bothered to know what to do, when the sound of the wheels of a cart some way off suggested a way out of the difficulty. Most likely the people in the cart would be market people going home, and all I need do was to get out of the way and leave them to find Smith and look after him.

I listened to the wheels till I was sure that they had not turned off towards Carter's Ford, but were really coming towards me, and then I ran to a bit of hill that hid me from where Smith lay, and looked cautiously over the top of the hill without showing myself.

From this point of observation I saw a cart stop when it reached Smith, and saw two people get out of it and go up to him, and presently saw them lift him into it and drive off towards Gower. Then, feeling there was no need for me to trouble myself further about him, I set off to find the missing donkey as soon as possible, fearing that my being out so long might already have made father and mother think something was wrong with me.

I soon found the donkey, grazing quietly with one of its friends, and took it home. Father asked me what had kept me so long, and I said I had had to hunt over the best part of the moor to find the donkey, as it had strayed far, and, as he was very sleepy he was quite satisfied with my story, and

only said that he should have to hobble the donkey if it took
to straying like that.

I was very glad that father was not more than half awake,
for the fright and excitement I had had made me feel queer,
and, if he had asked me many questions, he must certainly
have guessed that something unusual had happened. It
seemed extraordinary to me to find them all so quiet at home,
and I almost wondered that they could not see what I was
thinking of marked on my face.

I got very little sleep that night, for my head was full of the
robbery, and I kept going over it again and again in my mind,
fancying I could hear the blows struck on Smith's head and
could see the dreadful dark figure with the white face and
the shining pool lying close to me. Then I restlessly speculated
on whether the robbers would be found out; and what they
had done with the saddle and bridle; and what the mysterious
parcel could be which Smith had set such store by; and what
Tom would do with his share of the money. I could not help
hoping that Martha would not take any present from him
for a long time to come, for it would be stained with Smith's
blood; and yet I should not be able to tell her so. Then Miss
Gwenllian came into my thoughts and I wondered if I had
that night acted as she would have had me do. As to that I
could not be quite sure, because, though she had said clearly
that I was not to rob or murder, yet she had never told me
what I ought to do if I should see another person engaged
in robbing and murdering, and have no power to stop it. At
all events, I had not knowingly done anything to vex her; and
that was a comfort, for I had a queer kind of fancy that at
some time or other she might quite suddenly be able to see
me or know what I was doing when I least expected it; and
I used to like to think that if so, she would find me just as
anxious to please her as if I knew she were there; so that
those soft brown eyes of hers, which I thought of so often

and longed so much to see again, should look kindly at me. If only I had known that a day was coming when I was to make those eyes shed bitter tears, I believe I should have killed myself at once.

I wonder whether my worship of her and longing for her gave my mind any sort of influence over hers – whether my thought was like an invisible thread joining our two minds together, and moving at one end when pulled at the other; so that at the moment that I thought most intensely about her, she would also have some passing recollection of me?

CHAPTER VI

Next day I was wild to hear what had become of Smith, and whether he were alive or dead; but news travelled slowly amongst us in those times, and it was two or three days before I heard a word about him.

Then came a report that on last Sunday morning his horse had appeared at his farm without either saddle, bridle, or rider; and that this, joined to his non-appearance, had made his wife anxious, so that she had begun inquiring after him in all directions. Hearing that old William Rees and his wife, who lived on the Gower side of Fairwood, had been coming home very late on the Saturday night, and had found a man stunned and bleeding on the moor and had taken him to their house, where he had lain ever since without coming to his senses, Mrs Smith went straight there and found, as she feared, that the wounded man was her husband.

This was all we heard at first; but it was not long before another report reached us saying that Mrs Smith was going to send for the police, and have everything cleared up, and the guilty persons punished, directly her husband should be able to speak. But on the next day it was known that Smith was dead, and that he had never spoken a word nor seemed sensible from the moment that he was picked up on the road.

Then came the coroner, and an inquest was held, and the police went poking and prying about right and left, and a deal of fuss was made.

One of the constables came to pay Upper Killay a visit. First he went to The White Swan when no one was in except Jane, who did nothing but stare at him without answering his questions. But presently Phil came in, and from him the policeman heard that Smith had been at The White Swan on the night he was murdered, and had left it after dark; but as for being drunk when he left the public, why Phil would not allow that to be true on any account; and it was only from other people that the policeman managed to find out that Smith had really been as tipsy as it was possible for him to be and yet sit on his horse.

Then the constable – the very sight of such a person was hated by everyone in the place – went into most of the cottages asking various questions. But he did not get any good by it, for none of the people to whom he spoke knew anything about the murder, and if they had, it was not likely that they should have been willing to tell such a one as him about it.

Last of all, he came to our house, and asked mother if she knew of anyone having been out on the moor late on the night of the Saturday before.

'No sure,' replied mother crossly; for she did not love the police better than any of the rest of the Killay people did. 'I was not know nothing of nobody being out after Evan, there, was bring in the donkey.'

'Oh, then Evan was out, was he?' said the policeman; 'and at what time of night was that, now?'

'Time of night, indeed!' returned mother, who was in the middle of washing, and wanted to get rid of the man and go on with her work; 'who was say it was night at all? It was some time in the evening as the boy was go out – I not remember what time it was, to the minute – but I think as it was not dark hardly.'

Of course this was not strictly true; but I really do not think she had noticed how late it was when she had sent me after the donkey. However, the policeman did not seem quite satisfied, for instead of going away at once he turned to me and began bothering me as to what the exact time had been when I was out on the moor. I was very nervous lest I should show by my manner that I knew something particular, or lest I should give any accidental hint of it, and I thought that the longer I could keep to unimportant questions the better, so I pretended to be extremely anxious to answer him quite accurately, and to tell him to a minute what the exact time had been when I left the house.

First I told him what o'clock I thought it had been when last I looked at the clock before I started; then how much too slow that clock had been a week ago, and how much too fast it had been four days ago; then what I thought the right time might perhaps have been when I looked at it; then what someone else had thought on the subject. Then I went on to guess how long the time might have been between when I looked at the clock, and when I started out from our house. And then I suddenly thought I might have been altogether mistaken about the o'clock, and that it might have been on the Friday – or perhaps Thursday – that I had noticed it, and not on the Saturday at all. And with all this, and some more of the same kind, I made up such a long and confused history, that the man lost patience – thinking I was making fun of him and keeping him there on purpose to waste his time; he thought, moreover, that I was not the least likely to be able to give any information really worth having; so he cut my story short and walked off in the middle of it, exclaiming: 'Well, well, 'tis no matter for your old clocks! You do talk, talk on just like the ticking of one yourself; and I shall not be no fonder of them for putting me in mind of you in time to come. I never see such a fool! To be telling me all about clocks when I be wanting to know about a murder!'

With that he left us – mother going to the door after him, to scold him well for poking his nose in where he was not wanted, and for daring to think that a quiet decent family like ours should have had any hand in Smith's affair.

'Policeman indeed!' said father, when he heard of the visitor we had had; 'what a fool the man must be to expect as anyone shall tell him what he do want to know! He do be paid to find out something – but if someone else shall tell it to him, then there do be nothing left for he to find out. Then he do get his pay for nothing, and 'tis the one as told him as should be paid instead of he by good rights.'

For my part I quite agreed in this opinion, and thought that if I were to tell what I knew about the murder, I should be meddling in the policeman's affairs and leaving nothing for him to do. Besides – if it was a pity that one man had been killed, would it not be a still greater pity for two more to be killed? as would be the case if Hughes and Tom were hung for murdering Smith, who – after all – was quite dead and could not be brought back to life by it. So I held my tongue carefully, and hoped that nothing might ever be known more in the matter. What had become of the saddle and bridle made me anxious for a bit. But when at last they were found it was in an old barn near Three Crosses – which turned suspicion rather there than on Killay. And at last, after a deal of fuss and prying, and peering, and inquiring, the authorities had to give up, and confess they had no clue whatever to the murderer or murderers.

All that could be proved was that Smith had sold a horse in Swansea, and received the money for it – that he had turned in to drink at every public that he passed from Swansea to Killay – and that he had been quite tipsy on leaving The White Swan.

After that nothing was known about him till William Rees and his wife found him upon the road with his pockets picked and quite insensible – in which state he remained until he died. One thing which came out at the inquest set me thinking a good deal; and that was, that Mrs Smith said that her husband had no watch with him on the day he was robbed, and that she was sure he had had nothing of any value about him except his money. This showed that she could have known nothing of the mysterious gift that he said had been trusted to him for her; and so, whatever it was, it was something unexpected on her part. I felt thoroughly convinced that it must have been in the parcel that Hughes had ripped slyly from Smith's coat and kept hidden from Tom, and I wondered very much what it could possibly have been. My fancy was quite taken up with thinking of that parcel, and speculating on what could have been in it – but I had no chance of finding out except by asking Hughes, and as I dared not do that, I had to get on without knowing.

I would far rather never have seen what I had seen on that Saturday night, for it was long before I could get it out of my head at all, and I used to have bad dreams about it. It would have been a comfort to me if I could have talked about it to anyone else, but of course that was impossible; so I had to keep my secret altogether to myself, thinking that Hughes and Tom had a great advantage over me in being able to speak to one another about it, even though I would not willingly have had on my conscience what they had on theirs: so that in that way I was the best off of the three. I wonder if they used to dream of it as I did!

However, by degrees I got to think less and less of the murder, and one thing that helped me to forget it was picking up a new friend one day, in an odd sort of way, in Swansea.

Mother had sent me to buy some things for her, and I was standing about in the market when I happened to notice a boy who somehow seemed to bring Miss Gwenllian to my mind. He was pale and thin, as if he were half-starved, and was dressed in nothing but rags. He had nothing to do, for he was neither buying, nor selling, nor begging, nor picking pockets – as far as I could see – and he seemed nervous and uneasy, and kept constantly looking round, as if he were afraid of someone or something. I felt curious as to what he was doing, and what made him so restless; and whilst I was watching him he suddenly looked thoroughly scared, and dropped on to his hands and knees, as if to keep out of some person's sight, and pretended to be searching for something on the ground, and presently crept behind a barrowful of vegetables that was close to me.

I had taken to him from the first moment I had set eyes on him, so I stooped over the barrow, and said, in a low voice: 'I do think as you was want to hide from someone; shall you like for me to help you?'

He looked startled at my speaking to him, but nodded assent, and made a sign to me to stand in front of the barrow, so as to conceal him better. This I did; and, in a few minutes, he seemed to think the danger was over, for he stood upright again, and thanked me for helping him. I asked him who he was afraid of. He said that he had been very badly treated on board of a vessel, and had run away from her some days ago, and that what had frightened him just now was seeing one of the crew pass through the market. He said he was trying to get work, and had come to the market in hopes of finding someone to employ him, but that he had not succeeded, so far. Remembering that there was a farmer near Killay who, I knew, was wanting a boy to mind his sheep, I told my new acquaintance of this, and said I would take him to the farmer as soon as I had finished my business in the market, and that very likely he might get the place if he liked.

He would rather have gone at once, so as to get away from the risk of meeting anyone who knew him; but I was not quite ready then, so he had to wait for me, whether he liked it or not. He seemed distrustful of me at first – watching me sharply, as if he expected me to betray him, and looking ready to take to his heels at a moment's notice. But by-and-by he seemed to have more confidence in me, especially when he found that I shared my dinner with him; for no one can distrust a person who has given him food when he is famishing with hunger – not for the next hour or so at least.

I had finished what I had to do, and was just ready to start homewards, when a rough-looking man, in sailor's dress, came in at one of the market-gates, near where we were; and, on seeing him, the boy appeared desperately frightened and whispered to me: 'There is my old captain! Whatever shall I do if he shall see me? Watch you to see if he do come this way, and I shall crouch down out of sight.'

The sailor sauntered along from stall to stall, and seemed to be more occupied in looking around him than anything else, which made me suspect he might be in search of my new acquaintance. Presently he went up to a policeman and began speaking to him, and this made me still more suspicious of him, and still more alarmed for the boy's safety.

Close to the wall where we were standing there was a large dust-heap, and against this I told the boy to crouch himself as tightly as possible, and then I slipped a sack over him, and went nearer to the sailor to hear what he and the constable were talking about. Just as I got to them the latter was saying: 'Well, indeed, now and I should not wonder but what your mate may be right in thinking he was see the boy in the market today. There was a boy here as was very like what you do say, whatever. Why I was see him up by John Jones's stall there, maybe half an hour back. Come you with me, and us shall look if he do be there now.'

John Jones's stall was not far from where I had left the boy, so I slipped back through the crowd to where he was crumped up against the dust-heap, sat down on the sack that covered him, took out my knife and a turnip, and began peeling it, cutting it into slices, and eating them as calmly as could be. There I sat without moving, while the sailor and the policeman were searching about close to me. The policeman spoke to me, describing the boy upon whom I was sitting at that moment, and asking me if I had seen him lately anywhere near there. To which I replied that I didn't bother myself to notice what became of all the ragged boys in the market – that it didn't matter to me – and that I left it to those whose business it was to look after them. So he got nothing out of me, and I had the pleasure – for the second time in my life – of feeling that I might have helped a policeman, if I had chosen, and had *not* done it. After searching for some time the two men came to the conclusion that the boy had gone out by some other gate, and that they had lost him. But the policeman did not seem quite sure of it, and said that, in case the boy might still be in the market, he would keep a sharp look-out himself, and tell the other police to do the same.

After that the sailor went away; but the constable established himself near the gate, looking closely at everyone that came in or out, and sometimes taking a turn towards where we were, as if he still doubted that the boy had ever left the place where he had last seen him.

This vigilance made it so difficult for us to get away unobserved that I hated the police more than ever from that time out. I did not venture to move when I had done eating my turnip, and pretended to fall asleep for fear the constable should interfere with me if I sat so long doing nothing. I managed to say a few words to my living seat, to tell him it was not safe to go yet, and that we were being watched; and there we stayed till quite late in the afternoon before ever we had a chance of escaping.

Then, at last, the constable was called off into the street outside for a minute, and no sooner was his back turned than the boy slipped from under the sack, and he and I got off unobserved, and made our escape through one of the lower gates of the market, and thence through the darkest, quietest streets till we were well out of Swansea, and out of danger of meeting anyone who would stop him. Then we could talk at our ease, and by the time we got to Killay I had heard all that the boy could tell me about himself.

He said his name was William Jones, and that he believed he was about fifteen years old. When first he could remember he was living at Neath with his mother, but after some years she had come to live at Swansea, and soon after that she put him as cabin-boy on board the *Nancy Jones*, a brig trading to Havre.

After two or three years of sea-life – which he much disliked – he left the brig and went home, hoping to be able to stay ashore. But he could not get any regular work; and as his mother was always unkind to him – grumbling at him, and saying she could not afford to keep him and herself – he went to sea again, in a barque called the *Pride of Towy*, which was bound to Coquimbo. The captain of the vessel was a rough, brutal, tyrannical fellow, who treated Bill so badly that he ran away from the barque the instant she got back to Swansea harbour.

Then he tried to find his mother at her old haunts, but heard nothing of her at first, till the keeper of a shop where she used to deal told him, on the very morning of the day that I had met him, that she had died about six months before. He had then, being penniless and friendless, gone to try for work in the market, where I had fallen in with him.

Next day I took him to the farmer I knew of as wanting a boy; and he got the place easily enough, as his new master did not trouble himself much as to the character of a farm boy. The next thing was to get him a lodging, and as I had taken a fancy to him, and had taken him under my protection, I proposed that he should lodge at our house and sleep with me. Mother made no objections, and so it came about that Bill Jones was established amongst us almost as if he had been one of the family.

The more I knew of the boy the more fond I became of him, and after I had known him for six months or so I thought more of him than of almost anyone except Miss Gwenllian. He was not at all like me. I was hot-tempered, quick, and impetuous; but he was very quiet-natured, and his blood did not seem to run at half the pace mine did. He was fond of me in his own quiet way, and was sure to be steady and true to his friends; but he did not care about me in the passionate, jealous sort of way that I cared for him. I never can believe that a steady-going, quiet person, who is never in a hurry, and who never gets excited, and who seems as he could go to sleep over even his favourite pursuit, can possibly feel and care for things as intensely as a quick, hot-blooded person, whose love and hate rush as fast and as strongly as water falling down steep rocks. I suppose there may be some few people who, with deep, strong feelings, yet manage to control them and seem unexcitable; but there are but very few such people; and I believe that most calm and composed folk are so because they have no strong feelings to conceal, and are too selfish, or cold-blooded, or lazy, to take things to heart much.

If there is nothing in the world that a man cares for much – why then what credit is it to him to be always calm?

Now Bill Jones was one of these quiet, gentle fellows, that seem like so many lumps of ice when one expects them to care about things – and he used to provoke me very often with his indifference. He had feelings in reality, only there never was any getting at them.

He soon got to be liked by all the neighbours, but the most wonderful thing was to see how Rees Hughes took to him – a cross, ill-conditioned fellow like that, who no one expected would ever care for anyone but himself! However, so it was, and Hughes, even when drunk and violent, was always sure to be pleasant to Bill; besides that, he used to want Bill to be with him a great deal in his spare time, and to be more in his company than that of anyone else. To this I objected, and tried to interfere between them. Was it not I that had first found Bill and brought him there, and got him his place and helped him? And was he not almost my property as a friend? Was it not only natural, therefore, that I should be jealous of anyone else trying to carry him off from me?

And, furthermore, I did not trust Hughes at all as a safe companion for Bill, and feared that if he got much influence over him he would lead him into trouble. For I had not forgotten what I had seen and heard on Fairwood, when he had inveigled Tom Davies into being an accomplice of Smith's murder.

One result of that murder seemed to be the helping on of Tom's courtship of Martha. He had made her quite a hand-some present of a shawl and brooch, with which she was much pleased, saying that he really must have turned steady and taken to save in earnest, or he could not have afforded such an expensive present.

My belief is that she had always liked him a little; but, knowing how idle and thriftless he was, and being herself of a prudent turn of mind, she had determined that he would never be able to keep a wife in comfort, and that therefore she would never marry him, and that she must be very watchful over herself, for fear of getting to care too much about him. But his show of money quite deceived her, and made her think he was really putting by something against housekeeping, and that he was going to become steady and hardworking, so she let herself see more of him, and listen to him; and then she became more civil to him, and would walk out with him, and by-and-by it got to be an understood thing that they were to be married when he could set her up in a house of her own. I, being behind the scenes, and knowing where Tom's money had come from, found it a hard matter to hold my tongue, and not tell her how greatly deceived she was. But it would never have done to tell the secret, so I had to let the wooing go on. Everyone knew that Tom had only to save some more money, and then the wedding would be fixed. One day, when someone spoke about it in Hughes's hearing, he laughed, and said, that of course Tom could save money again just as he had done it before. This speech made me uncomfortable, for Tom was a great deal of his time with Hughes, and I feared he would get Tom into some fresh scrape, and then they might not get out of it so easily as they had out of the last. I was wishful to know how much Tom cared for Hughes, and whether there was any likelihood of keeping them more apart, so I said to Tom one day in a joking manner, as if I was not half in earnest: 'Why, Tom, you do seem most so fond of Rees Hughes, as if it was he as was your sweetheart, and not Martha. Is it that you do want to learn the way to be out of temper from he? But I have heard say that a man had no need to learn that when he is going to get married, for that his wife shall teach it to him, for sure.'

Tom, however, did not seem best pleased with me for laughing at his friendship for Hughes.

'What if I do like him?' said he rather crossly; 'what shall you have to say against it? He be so good as any other fellow in the place, I do think, for all your jabber about bad tempers! And I do think it is no odds to you whoever my friends may be, neither.'

I had no more to say, and not long afterwards Tom and Hughes went off together quite unexpectedly. No one knew a word about their going till Tom came up to our house to say goodbye to Martha. She was out at the time, and I think he would have liked to wait till she came in again, only Hughes was impatient and hurried him off; so he left a message with me to tell her that he might not be back for a week or ten days, as he and Hughes had heard of some work with good pay, and were off to try and secure the job, which was some distance off.

A week – ten days – two weeks – three weeks passed, and still they did not return. Then Martha began to fret a little after her young man – though no one else troubled their heads as to what had become of them; for the life or death of a poor man who has no family depending on him seems to make but very little difference in the world.

Several weeks after they had gone I happened to go into Swansea one day and heard people talking a great deal of a robbery at Neath. A house had been broken into in the night and a lot of money had been taken out of a desk in a room downstairs, and it had been managed so cleverly that nothing had been known of it till next morning. The police had no clue to the burglars as yet, but people thought they might have been gipsies, as a gipsy encampment had been passing near Neath.

I did not happen to speak of this burglary to anyone except Bill Jones until two days afterwards, when Jenkin Thomas began telling us all about it at The White Swan as a great piece of news. The first man to tell a story is generally credited with knowing it right, I have noticed, and if anyone else tells it at all differently the hearers pooh-pooh him, and prefer trusting to the man who originally brought it to them. So when I heard Jenkin Thomas saying that the burglary had probably been done by a man in spectacles, with a long beard and yellow hair, who had been seen hanging about the house for some time past, then I was vexed that I had not told the story my way first – for *my* story was that gipsies were supposed to have been the thieves; and who ever heard of a gipsy with spectacles and long yellow hair? I told Jenkin that he was wrong, and that I must know best, as I had heard of it two days before him. But he set up to know more about the matter than I did, and we were having a pretty hot argument about it when all of a sudden Rees Hughes walked in to the public, and the sight of him made us forget our argument, as we wanted to know when he had come back, and where Tom was, and how their work had paid, and so on. Hughes was just the same as ever – not wasteful of words or civility – but he condescended to inform us that he was only just back, that the work had proved a good paying job, and that Tom was most likely 'gone to see his dear Martha.'

I left The White Swan soon and went home, where, as I expected, I found Tom sitting in the kitchen and making eyes at Martha while she got supper ready. He did not tell us much about the job he had had – only saying that it had paid very well, and that it had been some sort of navvy's work at a place where the work had to be finished in a hurry.

He was in great spirits, and told Martha he would soon have money enough to marry her now, and as he said that he tried to get hold of her hand. But she was not in the humour for that just then, so she managed to upset a dish of hot potatoes over the floor, and kept him picking them up for her for the next five minutes. Whereby he burnt his fingers not a little, and was prevented from saying anything more about marriage for that evening at all events.

CHAPTER VII

It would have well for us – as time was to show – if Tom
Davies had been Martha's only admirer. There was another,
however, one Pugh Morgan, who lived at Lower Killay, and
who was an ugly, red-haired little cobbler, with a strangely
squeaky voice that no one could forget if he had once heard
it. He did not work very much at his trade, and was seldom
at home for very long together; he was constantly roving
away somewhere or other, and was often to be met with at
fairs and sales, for he had such a quick, sure eye for all kinds
of animals that farmers and dealers frequently employed him
to buy for them. For my part, I had never been fond of him
since once when he had behaved to me in what I considered
a shabby way about a pair of boots. As for Martha, she had
not returned his admiration of her at any time; and since she
had come to an understanding with Tom, she had never
looked at Pugh nor spoken to him; in consequence of which
he hated Tom cordially, and never lost a chance of speaking
ill of him.

However, I did not dislike Pugh enough to be unwilling
to travel in his company one day about the end of 1842, when
we both chanced to be going to a fair at Carmarthen, it being
then about two years since Miss Gwenllian had left Penfawr,
and I having grown into a tall, strong fellow of twenty.

A fair is a wonderful place for meeting people from all
parts of the country, and whilst we were standing together,
speaking to one and another of those we knew, and looking
at what was going on, a man whom I had never seen before
came up to Pugh and talked to him a bit, and then they went

off together, leaving me alone. By-and-by I met them again, coming out of a small inn, and I noticed that the stranger looked hard at me whilst I spoke to Pugh, and as I went away from them I fancied I heard him asking who I was. Towards evening Pugh came looking for me, and asked me if I would like to go to a meeting that night at which one Thomas Beynon, who was a first-rate speaker, was going to speak about something very important to us all. I wanted to know who Beynon was, and what he was going to speak about? Pugh answered that Beynon was the stranger I had seen him with in the day, that he had taken a fancy to my appearance, and had told Pugh to offer to bring me to the meeting if I would swear not to say a word about what I should hear there, for Beynon wanted to speak about a great injustice that was being done to us; but it must be kept secret from the magistrates, who would be all against him, and very likely shut him up if they could get hold of him. That the magistrates should be against the meeting did not make me at all averse to going there, for the magistrates, to me and to most poor people, simply meant rich people who were in power, and who made laws to suit themselves, and then sent anyone who broke those laws to prison. It meant people who let us poor folk come into the world, and live in it, and suffer in it, and leave it, without so much as knowing that we were there unless we happened to take the rabbits they chose to consider their own; or in some other way interfered with their enjoyments. Therefore their objecting to a thing certainly would not influence me against it, and as – like most Welshmen – I loved to hear a good speaker, I was very ready to take the required oath and go with Pugh Morgan.

We proceeded to a small public-house and sat down in the kitchen by the fire, till the landlord came up and asked if we chanced to have seen a coat on the road? Pugh answered, promptly, that we had seen one turned inside out. This seemed to be a password of some kind, for the landlord then took us along a narrow passage to another room, where from fifteen to twenty men were seated round a table, amongst whom I recognised Tom Davies and Rees Hughes. Beynon was at the head of the table, and as soon as we entered the room he said to Pugh:

'Well, and is your friend there' – pointing to me as he spoke – 'sworn not to tell a living soul what he shall hear in this room tonight?'

'Yes, indeed,' replied Pugh, 'or you may be certain sure as I was not have brought him here else.'

'Well, then, I will begin what I have to tell you, for I do not expect any others tonight,' returned Beynon; and with that he began making us a long speech in Welsh.

I soon found out that the injustice he was quarrelling with and that he wished to excite us against was taxation. After speaking against it for some time he said:

'What right have the Queen and her Government to put a tax on things that poor people must have? On the things without which they cannot live? And what do they do with the money they take from us? Who has it? Why the Queen has it! She and the people she chooses for her ministers! Are they poor? Or hungry? Or cold? Or naked? Not they! Rolling in luxury and riches – eating and drinking at one meal what would keep a poor man's family in comfort for a month – dressed in the best and finest stuffs of this country and other countries too. Those are the people who are not too proud to take the poor man's money to add to their own wealth – wealth which they fling away recklessly and squander on themselves, their children, and their friends, as though no better use than that could be found for the hard-earned pennies and shillings that we have gained by the labour of our hands and the sweat of our brows!' Doubtless the fine gentlemen think that the coins they wring from us are better laid out in procuring them strawberries and green peas at Christmas than if they were spent in saving some starving family from perishing of want! But that this should be tolerated is a shame, my friends; I say that it is a burning, crying shame!'

Here Beynon paused, and everyone in the room gave a sort of grunt – like there always is in chapel when the preacher is very moving – and we all felt, when we heard him put the matter before us as he did, that it was indeed a burning shame – as he said.

Tom Davies was sitting two off from me, and he whispered to me when Beynon stopped: 'I was not know for sure what be the Queen, Evan; was you?'

'Well – no – not to be quite certain sure,' answered I – also in a whisper. 'But you can see for yourself what a wicked one she must be for to have to do with such goings-on.'

'Right you are!' cried Beynon, whose quick ear had caught the whisper. 'If it is wicked to be greedy, idle, and to live upon the earnings of other people, and give them nothing in return, then, I say, the Queen is wicked, for that is just what she does. It is she who governs the country through the soldiers and police, who obey her commands. The magistrates act under her orders. If anyone is fined, or put in prison, it is to please her, and her name is on every warrant that is issued. Since her power over us is so great, surely her care for us should be equally great; the hand to help should reach as far as the hand to punish; but is that so? What does she know of you and me? Nothing. Does she come among us and find out if her servants are treating us well? No, never. We pay her taxes. What does she do with that money? She doesn't give it to the poor. With whom does she share it, then? Why, with her children, her husband, her relations, her particular friends, her ministers – with people of whom each one has already enough – aye, and more than enough – to keep him in what

we should call comfort for the rest of his life. But the evil must
be done away with by degrees; and I do not want now to talk
to you about taxation in general, so much as about one tax
in particular, one which we hope soon to compel the Queen
to do away with.'

Here he stopped again to wipe his face and have a drink
of water before going on with his speech. He spoke so beautifully, and was so much in earnest, that he entirely carried
with him all of us who were listening to him. It was all true
as far as we knew, and we had no doubt but what the rest of
it was true also. There was no doubt that we all had to pay
taxes some way or other, and that – well or ill – we never saw
a farthing of our money back, unless we went to the poor-
house. I remembered, too, having heard the Queen's name
read out in a police-court on a paper commanding a man to
be put in prison, so no doubt that everything Beynon said
about her was perfectly true. The only wonder was how we
had all managed to stay quiet so long while we were being
treated so badly! And as Beynon went on with his speech,
the grunts became more and more frequent, and showed how
completely we agreed with him.

'Look at the turnpikes!' cried he. 'Turnpikes here, there,
and everywhere, and at every turnpike an absurdly high toll
to pay. Does the money go to mend the roads? Nonsense! Far
more than enough for that is taken at the pikes, and little
enough do they spend on repairing the roads – the state they
are always in proves that for itself. The turnpike toll is merely
another excuse for getting money out of us; and I ask you,
friends, is it a fair tax? Does it press equally on all alike? Not
a bit of it. It does not press on the townspeople, it presses on
you – on the country people, who have to bring their farm
and garden produce to where they can find a market for it,
and who have to seek the market to buy the necessaries of
their own existence, and who spend so much on the tolls on

their road to the markets that they thus lose half the hard-won profits of their labour. And this unjustly extorted money goes to swell the revenues of the Queen and of her Government – to increase the luxuries of those who already have more than they know what to do with. Fellow-sufferers! Shall we bear this? England – miserable, servile, down-trodden England – may submit to such things if she chooses; but she is no guide for us. We are not cold-blooded English! We belong to Wales, to that wild Wales, which, in days gone by would be ruled by none but her own native princes, and long flung back every attempt of the English tyrant to grind her under his heel. Have we degenerated? Have we grown so mean-spirited and tame as to be no better than dogs that cringe and fawn on the master who strikes them? Never be it said of us that we are so unworthy of our forefathers! Let us now endure injustice and insults, but let us rise against our oppressors. Surely the spirits of our ancestors will be with us, and will encourage us to victory. Let us join together as one man and destroy every turnpike! Let our deeds speak for us, and declare that we will no longer endure the wrongs that have been done to us! Remember the grand old motto – '*Gwell angau na chywilydd*' – better death than shame, and cry shame on whoever is willing to be down-trodden, on whoever flinches from the task of helping his country to shake off her chains!'

By the time Beynon had finished we were all wildly excited, and were ready to rush to the nearest turnpike and pull it down there and then. But this was not what he wanted of us as yet.

'Wait awhile,' said he, 'till I can get others ready to join you. There are already many in Pembrokeshire and Carmarthen-shire, and other parts as well, that have sworn to stand this injustice no longer; but we intend getting still more adherents before we begin our work, and we might lose all by striking too soon. Keep yourselves in readiness to take action as soon as I bring or send you word that the time has come, and then, when every turnpike throughout the country is blazing, it may be that our tyrants will see they have gone too far, and that they must draw in their horns for the future in their dealings with the Cymry!'

We were not much pleased at the prospect of delay, for we were eager to do something desperate at once so as to let off the fury that was working in us. But Beynon managed to calm us down showing that waiting was really to our advantage, and promising that our waiting time should not last very long. 'A few months more or less will soon pass,' said he; 'and we shall strike all the harder for the strength we shall have gained during that time.'

He explained to us that he was occupied in travelling from place to place in South Wales to excite people against the turnpikes and to make arrangements to have a general rising against them as nearly as possible at the same time throughout the country. In this mission he now wanted an assistant, and he asked if any one of us felt inclined to go with him and give up our homes for awhile for the sake of this good cause. As for the others, he promised that they should hear how he was prospering whenever the news could be sent safely, though of course the great secrecy that must be observed in the matter would make the communicating of such intelligence an affair of great difficulty.

The moment he had done speaking I jumped up and volunteered to go with him. Two others did the same, and they were Rees Hughes and Pugh Morgan.

At first Beynon did not speak, but looked closely at our faces, as if he trusted much to what could be read there. Then addressing Hughes he said: 'I think by your face that you would be a faithful comrade, but I have never seen you before tonight, so I can hardly tell whether you are the man I need now or not.'

Here one of the other men exclaimed: 'Well, indeed, I can tell you this much of him; 'tis only about once in six months as he do ever feel real good-tempered, and by that time he do have forgotten how to show it. 'Tis for you to say if that is what you do like.'

There was a general laugh at this description; Hughes turned angrily on the speaker, and we had some trouble in keeping the peace between them. When the row was over, Beynon said no more about taking Hughes with him, but turned to me next and looked attentively at me. 'I doubt that you would suit me,' said he at last; 'you look to me too young, and rash, and hot-headed for what I need now. I would wish for none better when the time comes for fighting, but the man whom I take for my companion in the work I have to do now must be older, steadier, and cooler than you are. And so,' he continued, speaking to Pugh, 'there is only you left. Well, I know something of you already, and I believe you will suit my present purpose better than either of the other two'. Then he added to himself in so low a voice that I do not think anyone heard it except me, who was very close to him, 'Yet I do not know that your face reads the best either.'

After this meeting broke up, and on the next morning Beynon and Pugh had departed before I saw anything of them.

As for me, I went home again with Tom Davies next day, in a great state of excitement about the new ideas we had picked up, and looking fiercely at every turnpike we passed, and hoping soon to see it burning.

For a fortnight after that we heard no news, and nothing particular happened. I was dreadfully impatient for the fighting to begin, and longed to tell Bill Jones how unjust taxes and turnpikes were, and how we were going to get rid of them. But my oath kept me quiet, so I could only console myself by talking about it all to Hughes and Tom, who were not quite so frantic as I was, Hughes being older and less excitable, and Tom's mind being a good deal occupied with his sweetheart.

After a fortnight had passed, Hughes met in Swansea one of the men who had been at the meeting at Carmarthen, and this man told him that there were enemies about, and that we must be careful not to say anything about knowing Beynon, as the police were trying to get hold of him. This warning Hughes passed on to both Tom and me. A day or so after that a stranger came to our house, and asked if any of us knew one Thomas Beynon, and if he had been speaking in our neighbourhood at all. The stranger said that he had been told Beynon was a capital speaker, and that he was trying to find out where he could hear him, for that he believed Beynon's speeches were well worth listening to, and that there was a deal of sound sense in them. The man talked in an honest straightforward way that quite imposed upon me, and I should certainly have made friends with him if it had not been for the warning I had so lately had. However, I remembered that in time, and said nothing at all, while father and mother said (quite truly) that no such person had been to Killay, and that they had never heard of him.

Finding he could get nothing from our house, the stranger went to one or two others, and presently I saw him go into Rees Hughes's cottage. I knew there was no one in there except Hughes's mother, who had no English and was very deaf, and I did not suppose that any harm could come of that visit. But in this I was mistaken, for harm did come of it, though in no way that was connected with Beynon and his affairs.

The first inkling I had that there was anything wrong was the appearance of Rees Hughes that evening at The White Swan, in a very bad temper, wanting to know who had dared go into his house and meddle with his things while his mother

had been out in the garden? I told him that perhaps it might
have been the stranger who had been passing through Upper
Killay that day asking questions as to Beynon, for that I had
seen the man go into his cottage.

At hearing this Hughes looked as black as thunder and
went out of The White Swan as fast as he could without
stopping for even one glass of beer – which it was not at all
like him to do.

That same night he and Tom Davies went off together
without telling anyone why or where they went, nor when
they meant to come back. Tom did not go without coming to
say goodbye to Martha – who was quite put about at his
going off so suddenly and unexpectedly, and tried to make
him stay. But all her tears and entreaties could not keep him;
he was very much flurried and disturbed; and all he could
say was that he was obliged to, and that she must keep her
heart up and not forget him, and that he would come back
as soon as ever he could – or if not, that she would have to
go to him. He said that he did not yet know where he was
going, but that he was in a bit of trouble, and that she was
sure soon to hear what it was, and that she must stick to him
and love him all the same, whatever people might say about
him.

With that he went away. And the very next day we began
to find out what his trouble was; for the stranger who had
been with us the day before came back and brought two
policemen with him and wanted to get hold of Hughes. Very
cross they were to find him gone, and then they set to work
asking questions here, there, and everywhere, till they had
found out how long ago it was that he had been away from
home about that navvy job of work, and how long he had
stayed away then, and also that Tom had been with him. And
when they knew all this they declared that they were quite
sure that Hughes and Tom had committed the robbery at

Neath which I told you about in the last chapter, and that they were to be arrested as soon as they could be caught.

Then it came out that the man who had been with us the day before had been a policeman in disguise, and I do think that that is the very meanest trade a man can take to. For a policeman, who is the natural enemy of everyone, to go about in clothes that proclaim what he is, so that people may be on their guard against him, is one thing – at all events there is fair play about that. But it is quite another matter for him to go about dressed like anyone else, to try and get you to talk naturally and openly to him, and then make use of what you have told him to bring yourself or one of your friends into trouble. I never can understand how anyone can be got to take such work as that at all.

However, the policeman in disguise, who had gone from our house to Hughes', in hopes of finding out something about Beynon, had found no one in the cottage, as Hughes's mother happened to be out just then. The man had peered into some drawers and cupboards, on the chance of lighting upon any pamphlets or letters relating to Beynon and his plans – if such there might be – and in doing so had discovered something that excited him quite as much as if it had been what he was searching for. This was a bag, containing a pair of spectacles and a false wig and beard of long yellow hair. This policeman had been employed in the case of the robbery at Neath, and as strong suspicion had fallen upon some unknown man, with spectacles and beard and yellow hair, who had been noticed loitering about the house – sometimes alone and sometimes with another man – the policeman on finding these things made sure that he had got hold of the burglar he had been hunting after, and went off to get help, and a warrant for arresting Hughes. Meanwhile, Hughes, on coming back to his house, had been alarmed to find his things moved, though his mother declared she had not touched them; and when he heard of the stranger having been in the house he at once took fright and bolted, taking Tom with him. Lucky it was for them that they had got off so quickly; and very cross the police were to have missed them, and not to be able to get any clue to their whereabouts.

That night at The White Swan there was a deal of speculation as to where Hughes and Tom had taken themselves off to, some suggesting North Wales, some Devonshire, and some that they were hiding somewhere close by. But my own private idea was that they were very likely to have tried to join Beynon and his friends, for I was sure they both meant to help in the rising against the turnpikes whenever it should come off. Of course I had to keep this idea to myself, as none of the others were in the secret.

When I went home from the public-house I found poor Martha in a terrible way about the whole affair – and no wonder. Thinking that Tom was really getting to be hard-working, and steady, and saving money, and that he would soon have enough to marry on; and having therefore indulged the liking she had always had for him, till she had grown as fond of him as he was of her, she could not change herself now and make herself indifferent to him as she had been before. In love with him she was, and in love with him she would continue to be, even though his fancied industry and thrift should prove to be a mere dream. And now the police were after him, and it was impossible to say when she would be able to see him again in safety, and all her hopes of happiness seemed at an end. Bill and I (who slept in the same room together) heard her sobbing after we had gone to bed; and by-and-by Bill said, in a very low voice, so that no one else should hear him:

'Evan, be you asleep?'

'No, Bill,' said I. 'What is it?'

'Well,' he replied, 'I was think about Tom, and about what

he shall do. If he was a wise man he was keep away from here; but I think maybe as he may get wanting to see Martha some day and be coming back here for that, and then there shall be risk he do be caught. Was not you think the same?'

'Well, indeed, 'tis likely, too,' answered I, considering the matter; 'but us can do nothing to help it now, Bill, can us?'

'No,' he said; 'only I was think it was best to speak of it to you, so that you may be on the look-out if so be as he *do* turn up here. There's glad I am that 'tis not you as has had to run, Evan.'

He so seldom showed any strong liking for anyone that his saying so much as this surprised me, and being still half jealous of Hughes, I said:

'Was you rather it was Hughes in trouble than me?'

'He can mind himself better nor you can,' replied Bill, 'and he shall get on where you shall never get on at all. Besides, you was not think that I was care more about he than about you, Evan, was you?'

I was ashamed to tell Bill that I really had doubted that; yet to hear from his own lips that he cared for me was a great pleasure to me, for he never showed it, and it is weary work to be fond of a person who never gives any sign of difference between you and anyone else in their affection. Indeed I doubt whether I should have gone on caring for Bill as I did if it had not been for the strange way in which he often reminded me of Miss Gwenllian.

As I settled myself off to sleep, I wondered whether his affection for me would make him anxious on my account whenever the much-desired order should come to rise and destroy the turnpikes. But then I felt sure that he would join heartily with us so soon as he should hear about our grievances, and so, whatever happened, we were sure to be together. And, reflecting on this, I went to sleep.

CHAPTER VIII

That meeting at Carmarthen made a great change to me. Till then I had spent my life quietly enough; but now I was burning with impatience to begin fighting against a grievance which I had borne all my life without ever finding out that it was a grievance till Beynon told me so. For, however wrong the turnpikes now appeared to me, I very much doubt that I should have discovered their wrongfulness for myself if no one had put the idea into my head. I was so restless and eager to begin the fighting that I used to make myself quite miserable about it, as the winter passed drearily on and still no summons came from Beynon. I used to think sometimes that I should have been a great deal happier if I could have been as apathetic as Bill Jones, who never put himself out about things, and often laughed at my excitability – telling me that nothing came the quicker for being fretted after. Poor Martha, too, would have been better off if she had been more cold-blooded and had not been so anxious about Tom – for she vexed after him terribly, and began to grow pale and thin as weeks passed on and brought no news of him. The winter dragged through at last, and towards the end of March, 1843, reports reached us Killay people of a rising against turnpikes having taken place in Pembrokeshire the month before. We heard that parties of men with blackened faces and women's clothes had burnt and smashed many of the pikes – and when I heard of it, I longed to have been with them, and could not think why Beynon did not give any sign – why Glamorganshire did not follow the lead of Pembrokeshire.

But though I could not fight for the cause, yet at all events

I could try and get fresh adherents to it; so when the Rebecca*
rioting was discussed at The White Swan, I spoke out boldly
on the matter, and said as much as I could remember of
Beynon's speech – which I gave as though it were all my
own idea, so that I might not break my oath of secrecy or
get him into trouble by mentioning his name. Many of the
men agreed with me, saying that we had put up with taxation
and turnpikes too long by a great deal, and that it was quite
time for someone to make a stand against them. But two of
the men were much hotter for Rebecca than the rest. These
two were Jenkin Thomas, from Three Crosses, and Jim Jenkins,
and they came to talk to me about it privately – suggesting
we should get up a party and attack one of the pikes near us.
However, I remembered Beynon's advice, and so I preached
patience to them as he had done to me – telling them that I
knew for a fact that Rebecca would soon be at work in
Glamorganshire, and that we had better wait for at least a
little longer till I should hear when our friends were likely to
be ready. All that we could do as yet was to speak in favour
of Rebecca whenever we had a chance – and this we did until
I believe that all the men in the place had more than half a
mind to join her, and that if Beynon had then come there
every one of them would have gone with him. My father
amused me in the way he looked at the matter. He was not
at all against the rioting in reality, but he would not seem to
be in favour of it, because he was jealous of the importance
which I gained by having been the first to speak up for the
new ideas. He could not make out how I had suddenly learnt
to speak with reason against the pikes, and it vexed him to
think that he had never noticed the injustice that he had
always had to put up with, until it was pointed out to him by
his own son.

---

* The rioters who destroyed the turnpikes derived their name of Rebecca
from *Genesis*, xxiv, 60: "Let thy seed possess the gate of those which hate
them."

'What shall a boy like you know of what was best to be done?' he would say angrily, whenever I wanted to talk to him about Rebecca; so I used to hold my tongue to him on the subject. I suppose no father is pleased to follow the lead of his own son.

Jenkin Thomas, and Jim Jenkins, and I and one or two others, went so far as to get ourselves women's clothes so as to have our disguise ready so soon as the chance came to use it; but this we kept perfectly secret from anyone else. And we fumed and fretted to be at work when we heard news of the rioting creeping into Carmarthenshire, and nearer and nearer to us.

All this time Pugh Morgan had never once been home since he had left Carmarthen the morning after the meeting there; but at last, one morning in June, as I was passing to Sketty, I saw him standing at the door of his house. Of course I ran up to speak to him.

'Well, Pugh,' I exclaimed, 'so here you be at last! What news was you bring? When shall we have a turn at them old pikes?'

He looked nervously round to see if there was anyone about, and then answered in a whisper: 'Was you want to bring the police on us that you must shout like that, you fool? All I have to say from Beynon is this – I am to tell all friends to keep quiet for yet a very little while, and to be ready to come directly they be called. By August at the latest, he do say as Glamorganshire shall know what Rebecca do mean.'

'Where do Beynon be now?' I asked; 'and was you going to stay long?'

'Oh, I was not know where he is exactly,' he replied, 'and I was not go to stop here now. I do be on some business for he, and come to fetch something here on the way. I do have no time to stop.'

I should have liked to have stopped and heard all that he

and Beynon had been doing, but Pugh was evidently very unwilling to talk about Rebecca more than he could help, and seemed more nervous that I should have expected. Finding him so uncommunicative, and so evidently wishful to get rid of me, I went away and left him; and when I came back from Sketty some hours later, he had left his house, which was all shut up and empty as before.

It was not till July that I saw him again, and then he suddenly made his appearance at The White Swan one Sunday evening. He had been absent from the village for so much longer than usual that everyone exclaimed at seeing him.

'Why, Pugh Morgan,' cried one; 'be it you yourself come back at last? And what was you do with yourself this months past?'

'Indeed to goodness,' said another, 'he do have been away long enough to wear out more boots than he do make in a year!'

'Boots!' cried a third. 'Pugh do know better nor to go a-foot all this time; more like he have been making money to ride by spying out the best animals in the country, and trying to make them as they belongs to believe they be worth nothing at all, that he may get hold of them cheap, and sell them somewhere else dear. That is the way he do go on, I know.'

'Maybe he have been giving a hand to Rebecca,' said a fourth, laughing; 'buying the horses from her enemies, and selling them to her friends – was that it, Pugh?'

'Or getting horses for her, and cows for the soldiers to ride when they do go to catch her,' suggested Phil Jenkins; 'but, heisht now, all of you, for he to tell what he have been after.'

Pugh did not look very comfortable under questioning, especially when Rebecca was mentioned, but he tried to make joking answers, and not to show his dislike to the subject, whilst he stayed at the public-house. This was not very long, for he soon got up and went away, and then I followed him to find out what news he had for me. It was grand news that he told me. Rebecca had been very successful in Pembrokeshire and Carmarthenshire, and was going to begin work in Glamorganshire at last. Her friends were being summoned to meet on the following Wednesday night at a place near Pontardulais with blackened faces, women's dresses, fern in their caps, and whatever arms they could get hold of. There they would find Beynon and another leader, who would lead them against whatever turnpike should have been selected for destruction on that night. Of course perfect secrecy was to be observed.

I told Pugh what strong supporters Rebecca had in Jim Jenkins and Jenkin Thomas, who had already got their dresses, and to whom I had promised that they should have a share in the first pike smashing I should hear of; and I said I would bring them with me. But Pugh objected, wanting to wait till we had made a successful beginning, and saying that then men would be joining us fast enough without waiting to be asked, as had been the case in other districts. He seemed frightfully nervous now that the time of action was come, and was afraid of letting any new man into the secret. But I knew that those two were as safe not to betray us as I was myself, and that they would have been bitterly disappointed if left in the lurch at our first attempt at rioting; so, after a long argument, I carried my point, and Pugh agreed to my bringing them to Pontardulais; then he gave me the signal by which to know whether anyone I might meet on the Wednesday were friend or foe, and then asked where Rees Hughes and Tom Davies were, as he had to tell them also of the meeting. When I told of what had happened about them he was very much astonished; and I did not like him any the better when I saw how glad he was that Tom was in trouble and unable to come to Killay. He rubbed his hands, and chuckled, and exclaimed in his squeaky voice: 'Well, indeed,

now, and that do be capital! And so Tom do have come to
grief, and have had to give up courting the nicest girl in the
place. Maybe when Martha shall see no more of him, she shall
not think no more of him neither, and then an honest man
shall have a chance with her.'

This made me cross, for I liked Tom a deal better than
squeaky little Pugh Morgan, so I said sharply that Martha
was not one to forget an old friend; and besides, how was
he to know that she never saw him any more?

Pugh's face fell at this. 'Oh, ho!' said he viciously, 'then you
do be having Tom back on the sly, do you? Or letting his
sweetheart go to he for fear as she shall forget him? But take
you care, Evan; maybe some day the policeman will help
them find one another, and then they shall wish as Tom had
kept a bit farther away.'

I was sorry then that I had suggested to Pugh the possibility
of their ever meeting, and tried to laugh it off, assuring him
that we had never seen Tom since he left, and had no idea
at all of where he was. But though Pugh said very little more
on the subject, I saw by his manner that he thought I was
telling lies, and that I really knew more of Tom's movements
than I chose to say.

The following day Pugh was off again with Beynon's
message to some more of our friends. The day after that, the
Tuesday, Bill Jones came back from Swansea with another
great piece of news for me. That was that the Tudors were
to get back to Penfawr on that day or the next. I was very
much excited about this, for my impatience to join Rebecca
had never in the least interfered with my loyalty to Miss
Gwenllian, and I was eager to see her again, to hear her voice,
to find out if she was still as she used to be, or if she had
changed. I had often thought about her coming back, and had
settled in my own mind that if she were to be just as she had
been in the old days I could talk to her about what was

troubling me – about Tom, about Martha, about the injustice of the turnpikes and the necessity of getting rid of them – for that she should think rioting wrong never entered my head.

But what if she should have forgotten me? Or what if she should not seem to care about seeing me and hearing what I wanted to tell her? What likelihood was there that she should remember the rough lout of a boy to whom she had once been kind? That I should have thought of her and cared for her ever since she left was but natural, seeing what she was. But what was there in me that should make her think of me at all? Probably she had met plenty of other people who were worth far more than me in every way, and who would have put me out of her head. Yet, however rich, handsome, refined, or charming they might be, there was one way at least in which I felt I was behind none of them, for I knew that I would give my life for her gladly if need were, and not one of them all could do more than that at any rate. A man can love in earnest, even though he may have been roughly born and bred; and if he loves in earnest there is a chance that he may become in some degree like whoever he loves; so possibly my love for Miss Gwenllian, joined to her two years' teaching of me, might have raised me to some extent above the level of other Killay men. Anyhow, boy or man, I was hers wholly, and I knew that I never had given, and never could give, to any other creature the devotion that I gave to her. Very likely she would never know this, at least not on earth, but perhaps in that heaven which I believed in chiefly because she told me of it – perhaps there she might at last see all my life, and know how true had been my affection for her. Ah well! If I had not loved her as deeply as I did, I should not be here now.

Everything exciting seemed to be happening to me all at once, for that Tuesday night, as Bill and I were going to bed,

a pebble was thrown gently against our window. We looked
at each other in surprise for a minute, and then I said, as the
thought suddenly struck me:

'What if that be Tom, now?'

'Go you and see,' said Bill eagerly; 'but don't keep no noise
now to wake the others, in case it do be he.'

I slipped softly downstairs and went out, and sure enough
Tom was standing there. Taking him out of hearing of the
house, I asked him what he had been doing all this time. He
said he and Hughes had gone from Killay to Pembrokeshire,
where no one knew them, and had there joined Rebecca.
They had been knocking about with the rioters there and in
Carmarthenshire ever since, living as they could; and now,
hearing that Rebecca was going to begin operations in
Glamorganshire, and being very anxious to see Martha again,
Tom had braved the danger of the police for the sake of a
word with his sweetheart, and begged me to manage for him
to see her.

Accordingly I went back to the house and managed to get
Martha to come outside with me without anyone else noticing
it; then, telling her to be as quiet as a mouse whatever might
happen, I took her to where Tom was. She was so surprised
when she saw him that she tried to scream in spite of my
warning; but luckily I was ready for her, and clapped my
hand over her mouth in time to smother the noise at once.
She was quite quiet after the first surprise, and I left them
to have a good talk together till I thought it time for Tom to
rest, so as to be fresh and fit for work at Pontardulais next
night. Then I went and insisted on saying goodbye, giving
Tom some food for next day and sending Martha back to bed.
Very sad they both were about their prospects – and no
wonder – for there had been but little chance of Tom's being
safe anywhere in England since the Neath robbery; and now
there was fresh danger to him from his being concerned in

the Rebecca riots – all of which was a complete upsetting of Martha's original scheme for herself, which was to marry some thoroughly respectable steady young man, who would always keep a good roof over her head. She had never let herself fall in love with Tom till she believed him to be just such a man as she wanted; and now that she had found out her mistake it was too late to change, for she was so fond of him that she would rather have to beg her bread than to live without him.

The next day I went to Penfawr to see if Miss Gwenllian was come – but she was not expected till the evening, and as I had to be back in time to start for Pontardulais I could not wait. What a difference it might have made, and what trouble might have been saved, if only she had come home a few days sooner! For if I had spoken to her about the rioting, and she had condemned it – why I should even have kept away from Rebecca to please her!

That Wednesday was one of those lovely summer evenings when the daylight seems to find every part of the world too pleasant to be parted from, and when it seems to linger on into the night to the very last moment; and thus it was not quite dusk when Jim Jenkins and I set out from home towards Pontardulais. A little way on Fairwood we met Tom, and there we stopped to blacken our faces and put on our women's dresses in the soft July twilight. We certainly were a queer-looking lot of women with black faces, and beards and whiskers peeping out under the white caps. We did not much like the dresses, and felt extremely thankful that we were not obliged always to wear such uncomfortable costumes. I remember I thought the Welsh flannel bedgown I had on was the most disagreeable garment I had ever worn in my life. We were all three mounted – having each got one of the rough ponies that are always grazing on Fairwood. We were soon joined by Jenkin Thomas, coming from Three Crosses. He was dressed and mounted as we were, and – being always a bit of a dandy – had managed to arrange his bedgown and wittle so as to look quite spruce in his disguise.

'Well indeed, you do look like Rebecca's very best daughter,' said I, laughing; 'you do look as if you was never meant to be no better nor a woman in all your life – so there's for you, Jenkin.'

'Indeed then, and it shall not be hard for someone to look a better woman than you, Evan,' returned he; 'was you never look at a woman, you donkey, that you was not know how to put on a wittle better than that?'

And as he spoke he pulled off the shawl which I had twisted round my neck like a rope, and arranged it half over my head and half over my shoulders, as a woman would have worn it. But what wonder was it that I did not understand such matters? For what woman had I ever troubled myself to look at except Miss Gwenllian – who did not wear bedgowns and wittles at all?

We rode on without adventure till we got within about a mile of the rendezvous; and there we saw a woman sitting by the road who called out to us as we were passing her, and said she wondered to see young women out so late, and asked where we were going. I had been told by Morgan that this was the signal of a friend, and also knew what to answer, so I replied that we were going to our mother.

'Is she one Rebecca?' said the woman.

'Yes, sure,' answered I.

'All right then,' returned she, jumping up, 'she do be my mother too, and it is all safe. I was to watch here for you, if so be you be from Killay as I do suppose.'

Then the man – for he was no more a woman in reality than we were – brought out his horse from where he had hidden it behind the hedge, and came on with us. He was one of Rebecca's scouts, and said he had seen no signs of danger, and believed we should be undisturbed in our work.

On reaching the meeting-place we found about twenty men already assembled. They were all disguised as we were, and were roughly armed with sticks, pikes, spades, picks, hatchets, old swords, and whatever else they had been able to get hold of. It was too dark to see each other, and very little talking was allowed, so that I could not make out who was there except that I recognised Pugh Morgan and Beynon by their voices. Some more men joined us before long; and then a man, who had come to lead us, and whom everyone seemed to obey, made us a short address to excite us afresh against the pikes, to remind us how successful Rebecca had hitherto been, and to call on us to follow him to a pike about a mile off, and there to smash the gate and burn down the house. 'This,' said he, 'will be a just and righteous thing to do; thus we shall protest against tyranny and injustice, and show that we will right our own wrongs if no one else will do it for us. And now follow me, and keep perfect silence.'

There was a murmur of assent to this, and we were just moving off when it suddenly struck me that though of course it was quite right to destroy the gate, yet that it seemed rather hard on the turnpike-keeper to destroy his house and property as well. So – though rather afraid of speaking – I went to the leader and said: 'But, if you please, shall it now be an injustice to burn the keeper's house the same as the gate? And what shall us do if whoever lives there do try and stop us? Must we burn him, too?'

The man turned round on me impatiently. 'And who are you,' said he, 'who speak when you should hold your tongue? and who stop and argue when you should be hurrying on to work?'

There were low exclamations of anger against me from several of the other men, and I began to think I was in a scrape. But Beynon stepped up to the leader and whispered to him something, of which I only heard 'Keep the peace if possible,' repeated once or twice. When he had finished whispering, the leader said: 'For this once I will take the trouble to explain your mistake to you; but know better in the future than to think that Rebecca – the sworn foe of injustice – can ever be guilty of the crime that she detests so heartily. If the toll-gate is unjust, does not the keeper help on an injustice? If no one would keep a turnpike, then such things would cease to exist. But men are found who will do this for the sake of money, who are paid with the very money that is unjustly taken at these gates, and such men as these deserve to be punished. If they let us alone, we will do them no harm beyond destroying their houses; but if they try to hinder us, why then they must take the consequences!'

I had not seen the matter in this light before, and what he said seemed quite fair and reasonable, so I said no more, and we all set off at a quick pace to the pike, which we soon reached. Then our orders were short, simple. 'There it is!' cried our leader, pointing to the gate; 'see you that it is not there in ten minutes more!'

We rushed at it furiously. In a minute we had it off its hinges and broken up into small pieces – vowing that it should never again stop the way of a Welshman. Then the posts were torn up and demolished, and then we turned to wreak vengeance on the house.

Some of the broken bits of wood served for torches, and by their light we saw the face of a man, who looked almost stupefied with fear, watching us through a window.

'Get out of the house at once, you fool, if you don't want to be burnt alive!' cried Beynon.

'My house! my house!' cried the man in answer; 'all I have got in the world do be in her, and I do be a very poor man. Shall none of you pity a poor man?'

But his appeal was unheeded.

'You do have had fair notice – go now if you be wise!'

shouted one of our party, shaking a lighted piece of wood at the window, and then holding it to the thatch of the house.

The pike-keeper waited no longer; but, giving a loud scream, he disappeared from the window and in another minute came bursting through the door, and rushed away over the fields as fast as his legs could carry him. It was well for him that he was so quick, for the dry thatch caught fire like tinder, and the cottage was soon in a blaze. I do not think I shall ever forget how wild and strange the scene was – what with the burning house, the strange figures with negro faces and women's clothes, the fierce eyes glistening in the firelight, the smashed white gate, and the savage delight with which the broken pieces of wood were tossed on to the fire. I think we must have looked more like fiends than men.

But we dared not stay long. We knew that the fire would be seen from far around, and that the pike-keeper would take the alarm wherever he went; and that, therefore, the sooner we scattered and returned to our homes the better. So after a few words from the leader to congratulate us on our success, and to tell us to be ready to come at a moment's notice when Rebecca should want us, and to warn us to be perfectly secret about our movements, we broke up, and dispersed in different directions – Tom Davies going off with Beynon to a safer district than Killay would be for him.

How proud and pleased with ourselves we were as we went home! And what happiness it gave me as I laid my head on the pillow in the early summer dawn, to think that the first blow in Glamorganshire had been struck against the wicked people who oppressed us, and that I had helped to strike it!

CHAPTER IX

On the Friday evening after the burning of the Pontardulais pike there were a good many neighbours drinking at The White Swan, and Rebecca's first appearance in the neighbourhood was very much discussed. Everyone was in her favour, and as the liquor was drunk and tongues got loosened by it, many of them said that they would like to have had a hand in smashing the pike on the Wednesday before. Then one of the bolder spirits, encouraged by the general approval of Rebecca, called out: 'Why shall not us do better than talk? What if us was to get rid of one of them nasty old pikes near here – all by ourselves, now?'

There was a moment's silence, many of us being taken aback at the suddenness of the idea – but then came an outburst of consent and applause, and in a very short time we were setting to work to settle how the notion should be carried out, Bill Jones, amongst others, entering into the scheme as eagerly as it was his nature to enter into anything.

On the other side of Fairwood Moor, just before you get to Kilvrough, there is a lonely little pike far away from other houses, and this pike we determined to attack. Then came the question of when the attack was to be made. I wanted to do it that very night, so that there should be no possibility of anyone getting wind of our intention; but two or three of the others wanted to put it off till the next night, in order to get the help of several of their friends who they knew to be in favour of Rebecca. I urged that as the pike was so lonely there would be no one to go to the rescue of the keeper, and that, though not a very large number, yet that there were enough of us for the occasion. The others, however, amongst whom was Pugh Morgan, declared it would be more prudent to wait for more helpers, and in the end the more cautious party carried the day; I was outvoted, and it was agreed not to destroy the pike till the next night. The meeting-place was to be at a particular spot on Fairwood at eleven o'clock at night, where we were all to assemble, and then march off to the doomed gate, if all went well. I was rather uneasy, and so was Pugh Morgan, at the open way in which these plans were made before so many people; we tried hard to impress caution and secrecy upon them, and to make them remember there might possibly be some people in the world who did not agree with Rebecca, which in their excitement they seemed to have forgotten.

Next day someone brought us the news from Swansea that the magistrates were extremely angry at Rebecca for having ventured into their neighbourhood, and had vowed they would put her down, and were talking of calling out the soldiers who were quartered at Swansea. But we did not feel much afraid of them, for the authorities had already vowed vengeance against the rioting in Pembrokeshire and Carmarthenshire, but had wholly failed to stop it.

Pugh Morgan had come back with us to Killay on the Wednesday night after burning the Pontardulais pike, and he was constantly hanging about our house and coming in and out at odd times during the next three days, so that I half suspected he was on the watch to find out if Tom was coming to see Martha, and I was glad he was safe off somewhere or other with Beynon. For though I did not suppose Pugh would be mean enough to set the police on Tom – more particularly because in that case Tom might retaliate by denouncing Pugh as a rioter – yet still Pugh evidently bore ill-will against Tom, and I should not have been easy to know that the latter was in any way in his power.

Whenever Pugh came to our house he tried hard to make himself agreeable to Martha; but herein he entirely failed, for she could not bear him, and took very little trouble to hide her dislike, and – one way or other – always found means to get rid of him pretty quickly. One time that he came lounging in and bothering her to talk to him, she at once set to work to fetch in coals; then as that did not drive him away, and as he kept going back and fore with her, talking all the time, she found an opportunity to drop a heavy coal-scuttle on his toes – of course *quite* accidentally – after which he retired to rub his feet – swearing as he went. Another time he came in when she was sewing, and began telling her some stories – which he thought capital ones and had learnt with some trouble on purpose to try and please her. Down she put her sewing when he was half through the first story, and began dusting the furniture and scouring the floor till not a word could be heard for the noise and clatter, and he had nothing for it but to hold his tongue and go away in disgust. Coming in again when she happened to be making bread, he sat himself down in what had always been Tom's favourite chair, and began making eyes at her – looking up in her face with the most loving and insinuating expression he could put on. She would not speak to him or take any notice of him, but still he stayed on and on, persecuting her with his efforts at love-making till she really could stand it no longer. Pretending to want a jug from the shelf over his head she reached up after it, and in so doing managed cleverly to upset over him a basin of sour pigs'-wash that was standing on the shelf till someone should take it to the pig. It served him quite right for going on plaguing the poor girl as he had done, and I burst out laughing to see his face and hair and shoulders all streaming with the nasty stuff. He jumped up in a fury, for besides having the pigs'-wash all over him, he had been hit a good thump on the nose by the basin, and a blow on the nose will mostly put a person in a passion.

'You do think, Martha Williams,' spluttered he in his shrill voice, 'as it do not be worth your while to be civil to me! We shall see, girl, we shall see! 'Tis wonder for you to have a sweetheart at all if you do treat them all like this, throwing filthy stuff over them if they do so much as look at you!'

'And who do have the right to call himself my sweetheart unless I say that he is to?' returned Martha angrily.

'Oh, then! Do we never mean to have no sweetheart but one?' retorted Pugh with a sneer. 'And what shall us do when that one darling do be hung, or sent to Botany Bay – as you may take your oath shall happen so soon as ever the police shall lay hands on him? Maybe then it would have been better for us to have been civil to honest folk – like Pugh Morgan – instead of keeping all our kindness for an idle, good-for-nothing thief as dare not show his face in his own country – like Tom Davies now!'

This abuse of Tom completely finished out Martha's last remains of patience.

'Shall you mean to say,' cried she, 'as an ugly, squeaky, red-haired little thing like you shall be fit to compare with a man like Tom Davies? 'Tis time for you to know, then, as there shall not be a woman in the rounds as shall so much as look at you by the side of him! And as for me – you was never be my sweetheart – not if there was not one other man in the whole world. Go you away this moment, you little insulting wretch, unless you do want for me to throw this saucepan at you!'

With that she seized a great saucepan full of boiling water and potatoes that was on the fire, and if Pugh had stayed where he was for another minute he would certainly have had the contents of the saucepan over him. But he bolted out of the door as fast as he could go – only stopping to shout back from a safe distance: 'Very good, Martha Williams, very good! I shall not forget as I do owe you something; and Tom too! And don't you think but what I shall pay the pair of you some day when I do have the chance.'

With that he departed and troubled her no more for that day.

As soon as he was gone, Martha's spirit went too. She dropped into a chair, threw her apron over her head, and began to cry as if her heart would break – which vexed me terribly, for she and I were alone in the cottage just then, and I could not think how I was to cheer her up. After watching her in silence for a little bit, I set to work to clear up the mess of pigs'-wash from the floor; but still she took no notice and went on sobbing and crying. So then I stood over the pan of dough that she had been kneading, and began turning up my sleeves, saying: 'Well – someone must finish the bread for you, whatever; so I was try my hand at it for once.'

This succeeded in rousing her from her grief; for she was particularly proud of her bread, and never thought that mother or anyone could make it as well as she did, so she jumped out of her chair and drove me from the dough, exclaiming: 'And who shall be able to eat the bread if you do make it, Evan? Most like as it shall be nothing but paste. Why you was not know no more about it than a baby!'

Then after kneading and working the dough busily for a few minutes, she began talking about Pugh and his threats, and wondering if he would find a chance to do any harm to Tom, and fretting and worrying herself about it till I had a hard job to comfort her and cheer her up – promising to do my best to prevent Pugh from knowing anything of Tom's whereabouts so long as Pugh should keep up his love for her.

Having done my work by about six o'clock on the Saturday evening, and feeling restless, and not knowing how to get through the five hours that had to pass before we were to meet for work, I wandered about on the moor, and towards dusk I found myself in the lane that joins Clyne Common and Fairwood Moor together. Here I was standing when I heard footsteps approaching, and as I did not much want to be seen in that direction, I got over the hedge and kept out of sight. I soon saw three men coming quickly and quietly down the lane, and when they reached Fairwood they turned down to the west, towards the pike we intended to smash by-and-by. They were strangers to me and did not look like the people of the country, and I wondered who they were. As I loitered about I presently saw two more men come along the same way, and also turn down in the same direction – passing about half an hour after the first three – and their appearance, somehow, made me suspicious, and I felt uneasy lest our plans should have become known and our enemies be assembling to defend the pike. Before I went home to get my woman's dress, I saw four or five more strangers walking swiftly in the same direction; and now my suspicions were so thoroughly aroused that when I got to the place of rendezvous I told all the other men there exactly what I had seen, and asked if any of them had seen anything alarming. Then it appeared that at about nine o'clock Bill Jones had noticed someone passing by whom he took to be one of the neighbouring magistrates, who had an odd figure and stooping way of walking that made him easily to be recognised; and several of the other men had also seen people going over the moor in twos and threes. And these people had not looked like country people, nor yet like market people, and had all been observed to walk straight on, at a quick pace, without speaking, and though they came some from one direction and some from another, yet they all seemed to be turning their steps in the same direction – *i.e.* towards the very turnpike that we were intending to visit.

From all this it seemed highly probable that we should find enemies awaiting us, and that we should not destroy the pike without a fight. Whereupon the question arose whether to go on and have the fight out, or whether to go quietly home and do nothing for that night. I wanted to go on at all risks. Pugh Morgan wanted to give it up. I said that perhaps our enemies might not be in greater force than we were. Pugh said that as they had evidently divided and gone down in small parties, so as not to attract attention, we could not form the least idea of how many we should find, and our party only numbered fifteen. I said it seemed cowardly to give up. Pugh replied that he had always heard Beynon say that Rebecca had better avoid a fight, if possible, unless she was in a very strong force. After a considerable deal of debating, Pugh carried his point, and we agreed to let the pike be for the present; and so the intending rioters broke up harmlessly, and scattered back to their respective homes, in great disgust at their disappointment.

Pugh and Jim Jenkins, and Bill Jones and I, being going the same way, were walking along together, and by-and-by Jim said to me:

'Was you see anything of Tom Davies since Wednesday night, Evan?'

Pugh spoke before I could answer, and exclaimed: 'Was Tom at Pontardulais with us on Wednesday then? 'Deed to goodness, and I was not know it neither. Where was he come from? I was not see nothing of him!'

'Well, and no wonder for that, neither,' returned Jim; 'for when a man's face be black, and he dressed in a bedgown and wittle and bonnet, I do not think as his own wife shall know him on a dark night in a crowd, if he do hold his tongue.'

I did not at all want to be talking of Tom before Pugh, so I told Jim that I had neither seen nor heard anything of Tom since Wednesday, and then tried to get them to talk of something else. But it was no use, for Pugh would cross-question Jim till he found out all he could about Tom – that he had come to Pontardulais with us from Upper Killay, and that he had gone away with Beynon afterwards, and was pretty sure to take part in any rioting in our part of the country.

After Pugh and Jim had left us, Bill and I lingered out of doors for a bit – I cursing our failure, and fuming at it, and feeling myself much too angry and excited to go to bed. All of a sudden it struck me that I would go over to the pike, and wait there till daylight, and see if our enemies really were there. It was a little dangerous, perhaps; but, at all events, it would be a satisfaction to make quite sure of whether we had given up our attack for nothing or not. Bill said he would come too, so we just changed our dresses – as we might have to run for our lives, and the petticoats would bother us terribly in that case – and then set off across Fairwood Moor.

When we reached the other side we left the road, and got into the fields, and crept slowly and noiselessly towards the pike, not knowing but what we might stumble upon an enemy at any moment in the darkness. At last we reached a hedge very near the threatened gate, and hid ourselves cautiously in a great clump of brambles beside the hedge, and waited for the light to come and show us how matters stood. We had not been there more than half an hour before the darkness began to lessen, and then, bit by bit, the gray light stole in, and showed us the rough outlines of objects close to us. Then, as it went on increasing, we saw farther, and could distinguish the figures of five men squatting in a hollow of the earth, about thirty yards away from us. But though this showed us what we wanted to ascertain – that our suspicions had been correct, and the pike was defended – yet still we did not go away, some fascination kept us watching there to see our enemies depart, and we waited on for the broad daylight.

Presently we saw them get up and stretch themselves, and before long others joined them, from various other directions, where they had been posted to watch the turnpike on all sides, and give notice of the approach of Rebecca. They all were more or less stiff and cold and wet with dew, and cramped with staying long in one position, and we heard them saying to each other that they must have been called out on a false report, that everything had been quiet all night, that they did not believe Rebecca had any designs on that pike, and that they did not see much fun in spending the night lying out on the moor and in the fields for nothing. All this was amusing enough to us two, who knew so much more about the matter than they did. They little thought how near two rioters were to them while they were speaking, and how surely the fate of that turnpike would have been settled on that night if they had not been there to protect it!

At last they moved off – passing so close to us that we had to crouch into a ditch to keep out of sight – and when they were safely out of the way, we went home again – consoling ourselves for that night's bad luck by looking forward to a speedy chance of burning some other pike; as I was daily expecting to be summoned by Beynon again.

When we got to bed it was far on in the morning; but as it was Sunday there was no work to be done, so we both took a good long sleep after our night out of doors; and this made me so late that I could not walk over to Penfawr to try and see Miss Gwenllian on that day, as I had meant to have done.

That evening Beynon himself came to Pugh Morgan's house, where I, and the other Killay men who had been out with Rebecca on the previous Wednesday, came to meet him as soon as we heard of his being there. He said he thought we had done famously so far, and that when a few more pikes had been destroyed, no doubt we should get what we wanted, and the Queen would redress our wrongs. He said Rebecca meant to make a clean sweep of the toll-gates in the district near Pontardulais, and that we should be wanted to attack another one on the next Wednesday, not far off from the one we had already smashed. We were to meet at a spot some little way from Pontardulais, and wait there for the signal of all being safe – which was to be a rocket – and when we saw that we were to go on as fast as we liked. I asked if we should not bring with us all the men who had been ready to smash the Kilvrough gate the night before, and he consented willingly,

provided we kept the plan secret from them till just before
we were starting; so that we might not have another failure
through our intentions getting known.

Beynon was off again early the next morning; but as he
slept at Pugh's house it struck me that the latter must have
had plenty of time to find out all about Tom Davies's movements and plans, if he cared to do so. If I had thought of it in
time I would have given Beynon a hint to be silent on the
subject – but I forgot about it till after he had departed. On
both the next days I should have gone to see Miss Gwenllian
if possible – but something or other always came in the way
and hindered me.

On the Tuesday Pugh came to our house (where he had
not been since the pigs'-wash had been thrown over him),
and after some hesitation told Martha that he was very sorry
to have been so short in his temper when last he was there,
and that he hoped she would forgive him and think no more
of what he had said in his passion. Martha was quite ready
to make friends, as, for one thing, she never bore malice long,
and for another, she had an idea that if he was friendly with
her perhaps he would be the same with Tom.

Pugh stayed for some time hanging about the place, and
I fancied he had something more to say; but, however, he did
not get it out that day. Next morning, however, being the
morning of the day we were to attack the gate, he came back
again early, and, after a good deal of humming and hawing,
managed to say what was on his mind. This was nothing less
than to ask Martha to forget all about any other person she
had ever fancied, and to marry him! He put before her how
unlikely it was she should ever be able to marry Tom, who
would have to be constantly in disguise and hiding till he
should get altogether out of the country, and who would have
a hard matter to keep himself without being burdened with
a wife. Pugh vowed solemnly that if she would have him he

would always be a good husband to her, and do his best to keep her in comfort, and would never mind one atom that she had loved someone else first. And in time he felt sure that she would get to care for him as he did for her – and he had some very comfortable savings to begin house-keeping on – and would she not consider all this and give him some hope?

I was out at the time of this visit, but as soon as I came in, Martha told me about it, laughing at the man's impudence for taking her for such a weathercock as that, and saying she had sent him off in such a way that she did not think he would ever come after her again.

'I told him plain enough,' said she, 'that he need never expect for me to do what he wanted, not if he was to live till a year of Sundays do come round, and that I was mean to stick to Tom just as fast as he shall stick to me, and never be no burden to him neither! And, indeed, but 'twas something to see how cross little Pugh was look when he was go away – his face was most sour enough for to turn all the milk, I do think!'

No doubt it was very foolish of Pugh to expect Martha to change her love in this sudden manner, but then I do believe that at the time he was so set upon having her as to be quite silly about anything concerning her. It struck me that this fresh refusal would make him more bitter than ever against Tom, and that it would have been better not to make Pugh so desperate till Tom was safe out of the neighbourhood. But I did not worry poor Martha by suggesting this to her. The thing was done and could not be undone; and after all, I did not see that Pugh could do much harm to Tom without running the risk of having his own share in the rioting made known, so I said no more about it and began to look up the men whom I had had leave to bring to Rebecca for the first time that night, but whom I had promised not to tell of our plan until the last moment before starting.

CHAPTER X

On the afternoon of that Wednesday when we intended to
attack the second Pontardulais turnpike, Mr White, the chief
of the Swansea police, was in his office when he was told that
a man who would not give his name wanted to speak to him.
On being shown in the man seemed excessively confused and
nervous, and when asked what his business was would not
speak a word until he had shut the door carefully and been
assured that there was no one else within hearing. Then he
went close to Mr White and said in a low voice:

'They do say as you and some of the gentlemen shall be
wanting badly to know where to lay hands on Rebecca – be
that true now?'

'Yes, certainly,' returned Mr White; 'can you help us in the
matter?'

'Oh, well, no, not in my own self for sure,' answered the
man; 'but, indeed, I be not sure but what a man I do know
may know something about her; and I was think as you would
like if I could get him to tell you what he do know maybe.'

'Well, you had better bring your friend to see me, then,'
replied Mr White.

The man hesitated a minute before answering.

'For you to know the truth,' said he at last, 'I was think as
perhaps he may have given a hand to Rebecca himself at
some time or other – mind you, I was not *sure*, but I was *think*
so. Well, now, was you willing, if so, to promise as he shall go
free for himself for whatever he may have done, if he shall
come and speak to you now?'

'Yes,' returned Mr White, 'I am sure I can promise him a

free pardon if he gives us trustworthy information about the rioting, and enables us to catch any of the rioters.'

The man still shilly-shallied, and then said that he was sure his friend would never be got to say a word unless he were also promised that whatever he said should be kept absolutely and entirely secret. This also Mr White promised, telling him to go and fetch his friend as quickly as he liked, and to promise him full pardon and entire secrecy.

The man went to the door and opened it, but only to assure himself there was no one listening outside. Then, closing it again, and speaking hardly above his breath, he said:

'Well, indeed to goodness, and 'tis I myself as do be the man to tell you what you was want to know. Rebecca shall mean to attack the Pontardulais pike tonight, and she shall take a good lot of men to help her about it – they was be out in scores and fifties there I was think. And amongst them there shall sure to be that Thomas Davies as they was say was rob a house at Neath somewhile ago. He was go with Rebecca everywhere now. So now I was tell you all I can; and, indeed, if ever a one of the other men was think I was say a word about it, they was murder me for sure! So never you let them find it out, sir; and now good-morning to you.'

'Stop, stop!' cried Mr White, seizing the man's arm. 'I can't let you go away till I find out whether you have told me the truth or not. For all I know, your story may be meant to throw us on a false scent that Rebecca may have a clear field to work in somewhere else. You'll have to stop in custody for tonight, and if you have told me truth we'll let you go tomorrow morning.'

The man was desperately taken aback at this.

'They shall find me out for sure,' he exclaimed, 'and indeed and I do know they shall take my life for it! Let me go now directly and then I was go and join them as usual, and they was never suspect me one bit! Indeed and I was not tell you one word of lies – no, indeed to goodness! And then, when I was be with Rebecca tonight I was only make believe to help her, you know – I was not really strike one blow against you! Let me go, now, there's a good gentleman! You was not know what they shall do to me if they shall ever guess as I was come here to tell you.'

But Mr White was deaf to the man's entreaties. He promised that he should not be called on to give evidence against his late companions, and that he should be released on the next day if his story proved true. And then, after asking the hour and place of meeting, and one or two other details, he left the man in safe custody, and hurried off to take counsel as to what was best to be done, and to make all necessary arrangements.

It was a beautiful hot afternoon, and a cricket match was going on between Swansea eleven and an eleven from the country round about. Mr White – anxious to meet some of the magistrates on whom he could rely and ask their advice – went straight to the cricket-field, and found it crowded with spectators. One of the magistrates whom he wished to see – a Mr Williamson – was playing for one of the elevens, and had just finished his innings when Mr White reached him. Close by stood Squire Tudor, and also another gentleman named Powell and Mr White soon contrived to get these three away without attracting particular attention, and as soon as they were out of hearing of anyone else he told them of the visit he had just had – asking what steps they thought ought to be taken, and adding that there was no time to lose, as it was already late in the afternoon and the attack would be made in few hours.

'It's a glorious chance of giving Rebecca a lesson if only the story prove true!' exclaimed Mr Williamson. 'Do you think the man was lying or not?'

'Well, I hardly know,' returned Mr White; 'he was a shifty-looking fellow certainly. But he did not look very brave either, and I expect we shall very likely find matters as he said, for I doubt if he would have been brave enough to come to me with a false story in order to take our attention off from Rebecca's real field of operations – and there could be no other reason for his doing such a thing.'

'We must mind that Rebecca gets no hint of our knowing her intentions,' said Mr Powell, 'or she'll stay at home. Our trying to catch her at the Kilvrough pike last Saturday was a complete failure – she never showed at all – if she had ever meant to be out that night.'

'Yes,' said Mr Tudor, 'it'll never do to send a lot of men over to Pontardulais now at once; she has plenty of scouts, I believe, and we must manage to keep them in the dark somehow. Suppose we four, and seven or eight policemen, go off quietly to Pontardulais when it gets dark tonight? We'll pretend to be going to Llangafelach, or somewhere else, so as to deceive Rebecca if we meet her; and then we'll double back across country in time to be in at the pike before she has done with it.'

'Very well,' said Mr White; 'but if the man's account is true, there is likely to be a much larger force of rioters out than a party of twenty men could possibly deal with. It will be worse than useless for us to come face to face with Rebecca, and not be strong enough to strike her a good blow and capture some of her children.'

'Well, there are dragoons quartered in Swansea now,' said Mr Williamson; 'they might follow us at a couple of hours later. Of course it wouldn't do to have them with us, they would be sure to attract so much more attention than we shall do; but they might come up afterwards and get to the scene of action quite time enough to be useful.'

'Yes, I think that would do well enough,' said Mr White. 'I'll tell the captain to bring his men to Pontardulais so as to get them there about an hour later than the time when we expect the gate to be attacked. Then they can wait there until they are wanted.'

So matters were arranged; and accordingly seven policemen, headed by Messrs White, Tudor, Williamson, and Powell, rode quietly out of Swansea that night, along the Carmarthen Road, followed some time later by a detachment of dragoons.

And now I will go back to my own adventures; for it was not till long afterwards that I came to know of what I have just told you, only I thought it made my story more comprehensible to put all this in just at the time when it really happened.

CHAPTER XI

While a traitor had been thus betraying us into the hands of our enemies in Swansea, Jenkin Thomas, Jim Jenkins and I had been faithfully serving Rebecca at Killay. True to the instructions Beynon had given us, we said not a word about what was to be done that night until late in the afternoon, when we went in search of all the men who had been ready to attack the Kilvrough pike, and asked them to come with us now to Pontardulais. All were eager to come, and not one of our party of the Saturday before was missing when we met together to start except Bill Jones, who had unluckily been sent into Swansea on an errand for his master that day and had not yet returned, and who, of course, had heard nothing of the intended riot – as he, like the rest – had been left to be told at the last moment. I was very much put out at his not being back in time, as I knew he would be vexed at not being with us, and also I particularly wanted him to come, because one always likes to have anyone one is fond of engaged in the same work as oneself. I waited for him as long as I could, but it was no use – he did not appear – it was time to be off – everyone else was ready and eager to start – and so at last we set out without him.

We were all disguised as usual, and all carried some kind of weapon – whatever we had been able to lay hands on. I carried a gun of my own, of which I was very proud, and on the stock of which I had had my name marked, and one or two others also had guns. One man had a sword – another an axe – another a hoe – another a pistol – and the rest were armed with heavy bludgeons. We had ridden for a couple of miles when Jenkin Thomas suddenly said: 'Why where be Pugh Morgan? He was say he was come with us tonight from Killay for certain. Was you know where he be, or what be keeping him?'

'Oh, he was come to our house this morning,' answered I, 'but I was not know nothing of him since then. Maybe he was change his mind about coming with we, and was go and join Beynon somewhere in the afternoon – no doubt as we shall find him at the pike.'

'Was it about Pugh Morgan as you was asking?' said another man. 'I was see him go along the back lanes to Swansea way at maybe two o'clock this afternoon.'

At that time we troubled ourselves no more about the matter; but afterwards we remembered how he had not been amongst us when he had promised, and how he had been seen going towards Swansea at that particular time.

We went quietly on without interruption till we reached the place where we were to wait till signal-rockets should tell us that all was safe, and that we were to advance to join the rest and attack the gate. At this waiting-place we found some of Rebecca's children already assembled, and others joined us shortly. One of the newcomers who came from near Cwmbwrla, said that he had seen a large party of men riding along the Carmarthen Road out of Swansea, and this made us a little uneasy at first, for fear they should have been our enemies on the look-out for us. But then we knew that Rebecca always had plenty of scouts about the country, and that therefore, even if the police should be out, she would be sure to know of their movements and to be able to act accordingly; so we thought no more of the Cwmbwrla man's news, and joked and talked as we waited for the rockets to appear.

It was now past the time when we had been told to assemble, and yet we strained our eyes for the signal in vain. The minutes passed slowly by – it was half-an-hour late already

– and some of our men began to grumble and get impatient, saying that Rebecca had forgotten the signal, or that she feared danger and meant to do nothing, or that we had mistaken the night for which we were wanted. Then some of them began to talk of going home again, while others suggested we should go on and smash the gate by ourselves, and others were in favour of still waiting on where we were.

'I do be afraid in my heart as there shall be something wrong,' said Jim to me, 'and it shall be no better than at that Kilvrough pike on Saturday, after all.'

'Well, I do think it shall be worse this time,' replied I; 'because 'pon account we do have come so much farther, and there do be so many more of us. Why, I do think there be near enough of us here now to burn the whole of Pontardulais, let alone one wretched little pike, and it do seem pity to make fools of us by bringing us all this way for nothing. 'Tis just upon an hour us have been here, now!'

Just as I finished speaking the long-looked-for rockets flashed up into the air and called us to advance. We hurried on and were speedily met and joined by Beynon, and numbers of other men who had been, like ourselves, waiting for the signal at some distance off, and who now came thronging in from all directions, until there were about a hundred of us, more or less, as we marched upon the pike. I made out which was Tom Davies in the crowd, and, knowing that he had been with Beynon, who was in command, I rode by him and asked him why we had had to wait so long for the signal, and if he had heard anything of the men who had been seen going along the Carmarthen Road which also leads to Pontardulais.

'Yes, sure!' answered he, laughing; 'and it is police as they be, too, but they be far enough off by now! There was a couple of our scouts along that road, and when they was see the police coming they was think they was sure to be coming after us, so they was follow them and watch them. But when they was get to where the road do divide in two, the enemies was take the way to Llangafelach instead of the one to Pontardulais. So when our scouts was see them safe along that, they was ride in at once to tell Beynon as the coast was clear. He was think it best to wait a little and let them get safe out of the way before we was light up the country with this old pike; and so that was how you was have to wait so long. Most like as the police shall be safe at Llangafelach by now. Much comfort they shall be to the old pikeman there too! Why maybe he shall take them for we when he shall see them coming, and shall be frightened to death of his own friends! What fun if he was to shoot at them by mistake!'

We laughed at this idea, and at all the trouble our enemies were taking for nothing; but there was no time to say more, for by this time we were close to our work.

The turnpike-keeper took to his heels at once without attempting to defend himself; whilst we – believing ourselves perfectly safe from hindrance or opposition of any kind – hastily put down any guns or other weapons that would be in our way, before we rushed upon the great gate that stood solidly before us in the moonlight, throwing deep black bars of shadow across the white road.

We soon broke up the hated gate and heaped up the pieces by the side of the house, so as to make one great bonfire of all together – some of us laughing and joking over the work, while others uttered angry oaths and exclamations against the gate and those who had set it up. As soon as the pile was ready we set it alight, and just as it began to burn fiercely, I suddenly heard a voice call out:

'Mind yourselves now, men! The police do be upon us!'

I looked up in an instant, and saw some men galloping straight into the midst of us, and remembered in the same moment that I, as many of the others, had thrown aside our weapons and were unarmed. Luckily I recollected exactly where I had left my gun in a gap by the road, and ran back to fetch it as quickly as possible; but many of those who were in the same condition as I was, were too much scared by the suddenness of the surprise to remember their weapons, and could only think of saving themselves. They would not have been so cowardly, I believe, if they had had time to prepare for a fight; but the sudden shock of the danger, just when they had felt so secure, was too much for them, and made many of them lose their heads, so that when the police charged into the midst of us they fell upon a crowd of men of whom the greater part were panic-stricken, unarmed, and only eager to escape. I do not deny that it was plucky of our enemies to ride at us as they did – they being only eleven in number, while there were probably more than a hundred of us – but then they had three things which were immensely in their favour, and which more than made up for their small number. First – they were expecting to fight and were all ready for it, whereas we were totally unprepared at that moment. Secondly – they were well armed, whereas only a few of us were so. Thirdly – they were well trained and under command, whereas we were wholly undisciplined.

But though most of Rebecca's children disgraced themselves by running away at once without striking one blow for their cause, yet it was not all who did so. Some of us made a stand and fought bravely, notwithstanding the mob of terrified cowards who surrounded us and almost swept us away in spite of ourselves. As soon as I could get my gun from the gap where I had left it, I flew back to where the row was hottest. There was plenty of light – not only from the moon, but also from the bonfire we had made with the broken-up gate and house; for this was flaring brightly, and made everything near almost as clear as daylight.

The first person I recognised as I hurried back with my gun was Rees Hughes, who had got hold of a great hedge-stake and was striking furiously with it at one of the enemy. They grappled together and rolled over in a ditch close by; but as I knew Hughes to be strong enough to hold his own against most men, I thought it would be waste of time for me to stop and interfere there, so I left him to fight his own battles and plunged into the thick of the scrimmage. The first policeman I came to had got hold of one of our people by the collar and was struggling with him. With a large knife that I carried I made a deep gash in the leg of the horse on which the constable was mounted – ham-stringing the animal and bringing it to the ground. The rider had to let go of his prisoner, and tried to spring clear of the horse as he fell; but I struck him heavily on the head with the stock of my gun, and saw him sink to the ground stunned and senseless.

The next thing I saw was Jenkin Thomas struggling between two men – one on horseback and the other on foot – who were trying to take him prisoner. He was fighting like a lion, but the man on horseback – whose back was turned towards me – had just managed to seize his right arm firmly, which destroyed his chance of keeping off the other enemy. At this moment Jenkin caught sight of me in the bright firelight and shouted out: 'Help me now, Evan, can you? or they shall get me for sure!' It was not likely that I could see an old friend taken prisoner without doing what I could to help him, and even before he spoke my gun had been raised to my shoulder. Taking as steady an aim as I could at the man on horseback, I pulled the trigger. As I did so he turned towards me and I caught a glimpse of his face, and it seemed to me somehow as if I must have seen it somewhere or other before; but who he was I could not recollect, and I had not time to stop and think about it then. My aim had been good, and he threw up his arms into the air and dropped off his horse, thereby setting Jenkin free, and enabling him to knock down his other enemy without further assistance.

But the small number of rioters who had stayed to fight were not enough to win the battle, and many of those few had been overpowered and taken prisoners.

Just as Jenkin disposed of his assailant, Beynon, who had been fighting as bravely as anyone from the first, shouted out to us: 'No use staying longer! We're beaten this time. We must make off for our lives, and try not to be caught. It's all we can do.'

What he said was true. He and Jenkin and I were the only rioters to be seen who were still free and unwounded, and even we were so hemmed in by our enemies that we could not possibly have got away if they had not been encumbered by the number of prisoners they had taken. So, however bitter it was to us to have to turn our backs upon the foe and run away like cowards, there was nothing better to be done, and we extricated ourselves from the crowd of men and horses and set off across country at full speed, I throwing down my gun to make me the lighter, as it was now discharged and useless to me.

Two mounted policemen started after us, and Beynon told us to keep with him, as he knew the country better than we did. He led us first over a high, rotten hedge, then down a rough, narrow little lane, then across a couple of small fields, with awkward hedges for a horse to get over, and then down another dark stony lane, and by that time we had shaken off our pursuers, who could not ride over the hedges nearly as fast as we got over them on foot, and who also probably thought it unwise to get far away from their main body for fear of an ambush.

We ran on for some little distance after they turned back, and were joined by two or three more of our friends who had stayed to fight as we had done as long as there seemed a possibility of doing any good by it, and who were now also escaping. Presently we reached a large party of rioters who had run away at the very first moment of danger, and who had gathered there looking rather foolish, and debating whether to go straight home or not.

We were now at a safe distance from the scene of action, and Beynon, glancing quickly around and seeing how many of us were there, thought there was still a chance of doing some good and rescuing some if not all of our friends who had fallen into the power of the enemy.

'Are not you ashamed of yourselves?' cried he to those who had run away at first; 'are you not ashamed to think that you great strong men have run away, like a lot of silly frightened sheep, without waiting to strike so much as one blow for the sake of right and justice? Have you forgotten our motto – '*Gwell angau na chywilydd*'? Do you mean for the future to endure unmurmuringly every hardship and unjust tax and burden that may be the laid upon you? I don't believe it of you! It was only the first surprise that made you fly, and there is still time to show the enemy that he hasn't yet won the victory, and that Rebecca is not to be beaten so easily as he may think. Think of our friends who have been captured – shall we leave them to the mercy of their enemies? Or shall we go back and rescue them and wipe out the disgrace of our defeat? There are plenty of us here to make the attempt – who will come with me to do it?'

'I will!' cried I, and Jenkin Thomas, and pretty nearly a score of others; but the rest of the men were still too much scared to go back, and would not join us. So we left them to go home in safety, while we bolder ones followed Beynon back towards the turnpike – all of us with our blood up, and fierce at our misfortunes, and eager to be revenged for having had to take flight like cowards.

We went silently along till we reached a hedge, about six hundred yards from where the pike had been, and there we stopped and reconnoitred to see how matters stood.

The fire had by this time sunk into a red smouldering heap, flashing out now and then into fresh flame as some hitherto unburnt fragment caught fire, and lit up for a moment or so the surrounding dark shadows. But no people could we see near it, the place seemed to be completely deserted, and there was nothing to tell what we especially desired to know, viz. whether the police had already begun their return to Swansea with their prisoners, or whether they were still near where we had left them. As it was most essential to the rescue, we proposed that we should know this. Beynon and I left the rest of our little band to await our return, and advanced alone to try and find out. As we got close to the fire we heard voices at a short distance off. Guided by the sounds, we crept cautiously towards them keeping carefully out of reach of the occasional fitful gleams of firelight, till we reached a field, which contained a shed in one corner of it. In this field were the police keeping watch over their captives, whom they had placed in the shed, and one or two low groans from the shed told us that some of its inmates were wounded. However, if our side had suffered, at all events the other side had suffered also, and several of them were lying propped against the shed and the hedge in a way that showed them to be more or less damaged. The moon gave us plenty of light, and we were able to make out all this after very few minutes' observation.

'It is strange for them to wait here like this instead of moving off at once,' whispered Beynon to me; 'I don't understand it at all. Perhaps they are waiting for daylight to move. Let us creep a little farther up the hedge, and try and hear what they say.'

Accordingly we crawled some way round on our hands and knees, and then again peered through the bushes.

From the point of observation we had now reached we were in sight of an object we had not before seen, and which bore stronger witness than anything else to the stand that some, at least, of us had made before taking flight, for there, close to the shed, lying perfectly stiff and quiet on the earth in the moonlight, we saw the figure of someone who neither spoke nor moved nor groaned, and to whom no one offered water and such other help as they offered to the other recumbent figures – for the man was dead. The dead man's face was covered by a handkerchief that had been thrown over it, and the body was laid by itself almost behind the shed, as if the living had a horror of looking at the empty husk in which their companion had so lately dwelt, and shrank even from having it near them. The clothes told us that it was no child of Rebecca's; and Beynon whispered to me: 'Why, that is the man you shot! I saw you do it, and very neatly done it was, too.'

And as I looked at my handiwork lying there before me I felt a savage joy that I had put it out of the power of one, at least, of our enemies to go home and boast of how easily he had made Rebecca take to her heels. Whatever might happen afterwards, I should always have the satisfaction of remembering that I had rid the world of at all events one of those who defended injustice – and that if I had been forced to run away like a coward, yet that I had been revenged on one, at least, of those who had so disgraced me.

Beynon pointed silently to a hedge passing close behind the shed, and making an angle with a second hedge that ran round the next field beyond. 'We might creep up there with all our men without being seen till we are almost touching the shed,' whispered he.

I nodded.

'Then a few of us might rush to the shed and set free the prisoners,' continued he, 'while the rest tackle the enemy. We are nearly as many as they are, and then as soon as the prisoners are free they would add to our numbers. What with the surprise and hard fighting we might beat them still. Let us go back for the others.'

We were just turning away when a fresh sound caught my ear.

'Hark!' whispered I to Beynon, 'was you not hear something?'

'Only the wind in the bushes, and these men here,' replied he. 'Come on, there's no time to lose.'

'Stop you one minute,' I said; 'I did think to hear a horse galloping – listen you again.'

We listened, and heard nothing for a moment or so. But then the sound came distinctly and more loudly than before, and there could be no doubt of its being a horse's feet coming quickly along the road. Our enemies heard it also, and one or two of them went to the other side of the field and jumped upon the hedge to look down the road. It was not long before a mounted policeman galloped into the field.

'It's all right!' he exclaimed; 'the soldiers were awaiting orders at Pontardulais. They are close behind me and will be here directly.'

Beynon and I looked at each other in dismay. The soldiers! Here was a complete check to our hopes, for we had no chance whatever of effecting a rescue now. We waited to be sure that the bad news was true; and in a very few minutes more we heard the noise of many horses advancing in the distance, and the clanking of steel spurs and scabbards sounded through the quiet night air as a troop of dragoons came trotting up with their arms flashing brightly in the white moonlight.

Beynon muttered a bitter curse. 'It's all over for tonight,' he whispered; 'we must get away from here as fast as we can, for some of them may ride about to try and pick up a stray Rebecca or so now that they are in such strong force.'

We managed to withdraw unobserved from the field, and as soon as we reached the rest of our party, Beynon merely told them to follow him at once, and led them to a good distance away from our enemies before he stopped; then he told them what we had seen.

All those men were true and staunch enough, and had set their hearts on having another fight with the enemy as much as I had; their faces fell when they heard the bad news, and knew that we could do no more that night.

'Curses on them!' cried one man, 'and how ever did they come to have the soldiers all ready there at Pontardulais just in the nick of time?'

'There's only one way that I can explain it,' said Beynon, who was looking as black as thunder; 'it seems to me someone *must* have told our plans to our foes – they seem to have known so very accurately about our movements and our numbers – for I don't suppose they would have had out the soldiers unless they knew that Rebecca meant to be out in force.'

'Well, it *do* seem as if they was know uncommon well what we was mean to do,' observed another man; 'but who could have told on us?'

'Whoever he was I'd like to have him here at this minute,' exclaimed someone else fiercely; and there was an angry growl from the rest of us that the traitor might have trembled in his shoes to hear.

'If we *have* been betrayed,' continued Beynon, 'it must have been by some one of ourselves whom I thoroughly trusted. No one in whom I had not full confidence knew of the plans and arrangements for tonight until the last moment before starting – by which time it would have been too late for anyone to tell our enemies in time for them to prepare for us as they seem to have done. I only told about a dozen people beforehand, and left them to bring the rest of you in time to meet and do our work. And each one to whom I told the secret was a man who had already worked for Rebecca and committed himself to the cause. If anyone of them has played us false be deserves to—'

'Die!' interrupted a voice; and the word was repeated by

the others in a low and intense tone of bitter hatred. Then and there we solemnly swore that if ever we should contrive to find out who had betrayed us that night, we would leave no stone unturned to bring him to punishment – not even though he might be the dearest friend we possessed.

Tired, sore at heart, uneasy at the possibility of an unknown traitor amongst us, dispirited at our failure, and grieving over our captured comrades, we dispersed in various directions towards our homes. But our weary journey homewards was not as safe and uninterrupted as the coming out had been; for there were soldiers riding about the country in search of more prisoners and we narrowly escaped being taken once or twice.

They very nearly got us, once in particular. Hearing them coming, Jenkin Thomas and I had tucked ourselves away like rabbits in a clump of gorse by the roadside. When they got there one of them noticed the gorse, and said he should ride his horse into it in case any rioter might be hidden there. His companions laughed at the idea, and said that not even Rebecca running away from a redcoat would get into such prickles as that; but the man persisted in trying to force his horse in. Luckily for us, however, the horse shied at the thorns and could not be made to face them, which I – who was feeling their sharpness pretty acutely – thought proved the horse to be a sensible beast; so the man gave up the attempt and rode on with his friends, after making a random thrust into the bush which passed very near Jenkin's foot.

When we were safe from the soldiers I tried to find out from the men who were going our way what had become of Tom Davies and Rees Hughes, but no one could tell me anything more about them than that they had been seen to stay and fight instead of running away at the first attack. I asked also about Pugh Morgan, but no one seemed to have seen him at all; and I thought he was very likely to have been one of the first to run, as I had not a very high opinion of his courage.

I think the only comfort I had on that long dreary journey back to Killay, was to think how lucky it was that Bill Jones had not been with us, for I should have been doubly wretched if he had chanced to fall into the hands of the police; which might very easily have happened if he had been there, as he was too plucky to run away, and was smaller and weaker and younger than the rest of us. The miserable journey came to an end at last, and I found myself again at our house, feeling too much worn out and tired to have gone a mile farther for any consideration whatever.

Bill was very glad to see me when I got up to the room that he and I shared. He said he had been wondering what had become of me, and could not believe it possible for me to have gone to help Rebecca again without giving him a chance of coming too. Tired as I was, I told him how it had happened, and what a disastrous night's work we had had, and how we suspected we had been betrayed. He listened with the utmost interest and as soon as I had finished he said:

'Then what was you do with your gun after you was shoot the man? For you do not have her with you now.'

'Oh, I was throw her down when I was run off,' I answered; 'I was not have no time to load her again after she was let off, you see, and she was be in my way for running.'

'Well, but you was never go for to leave her there, was you?' he returned anxiously. 'Why, she was have Evan Williams, Upper Killay, cut on her stock as plain as could be. Was you not recollect how you was have it done one day in Swansea, and how proud of it you was afterwards, too?'

I started as he spoke. It was all just as he said, but I had forgotten all about it till that moment.

''Tis right you are, Bill,' I answered. 'But for all that I was never think of it, and I was leave her there like a fool! I must bolt then for sure, for so soon as they shall find her there shall be no more safety for me here. They shall see she is fired off, and shall see my name on her,'

'Well, I do suppose as there was other guns out so well as yours though,' observed Bill; 'so, after all, they shall not be able to tell from that who shot the man as was killed.'

I thought for a moment, and tried to go through all that had happened in my memory. 'I was not so sure of that neither, Bill,' I replied; 'for now that I do come to think of it, I was not hear any other gunshot but only that one. There was several pistols fired, but not another gun. No, if they shall catch me, they shall hang me I do suppose.'

Bill was dismayed. 'Oh, Evan, whatever shall us do?' he cried. 'Indeed, and I do think as it was best for you to start now this minute and get so far away as possible before ever they shall begin to look for you!'

But I was far too tired to move another step just then, come what might.

'There can't be no such hurry as all that,' I said, rolling myself wearily into bed. 'Maybe as they shall not pick the gun up for some time again; and anyways 'tisn't possible as I shall go any farther till I shall have rested myself first. I was start again when I was have had a sleep, but indeed to goodness that be the only thing as I be fit for now.'

So, careless of anything that might happen so long as I had a rest, I settled myself off to sleep with the daylight streaming in at the window, whilst Bill turned out into the road to keep watch for any enemies.

CHAPTER XII

When a man is really dead-beat he is hardly like his own self in anything. Life and death seem unimportant to him – he can neither think, nor speak, nor act, nor understand rightly for the time – only let him have quiet and rest, and then he is satisfied to let everything else go. But as soon as he has slept and refreshed himself he is his old self again, and cares for life and the things in it just as usual; and this was the state I was in after that night at Pontardulais. I went to sleep too thoroughly done up to care much what became of me or what danger I was in; but I woke at about two o'clock in the afternoon in a very different frame of mind, and fully alive to the necessity of escaping as quickly as possible. Furthermore I was excessively hungry, and on going downstairs to get some food, I was a good deal astonished to find Tom Davies in the kitchen with mother and Martha. They looked melancholy enough, for Martha was crying, and Tom sitting close to her and looking as if he were almost ready to do the same.

'Well, and I be real glad to see you safe and well, Tom!' I exclaimed. 'And what was become of you last night after the row was begin? Tell me all about it now while I get a bit of breakfast.'

Bill Jones was on the watch outside, so we knew we should have notice if danger approached, and so we were able to feel tolerably safe while I satisfied my hunger and Tom told me his adventures of the night.

He had done his duty in the fight as long as there was a chance of doing any good, and then, when there was nothing for it but to take to his heels, he was running across a field when the sight of two policemen coming towards him with a prisoner checked him. They had not seen him, however, and as there was a shed in the field he has slipped into it to hide; and, once there, it struck him he might as well stay there till the coast was clear, so he climbed up to the roof and stored himself away in the thatch, though it was rather old and rotten.

This shed chanced to be the very one to which the police brought their prisoners; so Tom was forced to stay in the thatch a good deal longer than he had expected. He said he got frightfully stiff with crouching there so long, and that he was in mortal terror all the time lest the half-decayed straw and woodwork should give way under him and expose his presence. From his hiding-place he had overheard enough to make him pretty sure that Rebecca's intentions for that night had been perfectly well known to some one of her enemies. He heard two men laughing over the pretence of sending the police to Llangafelach which had so completely deceived us and lulled us to a false security. He heard, also, that soldiers were waiting close at hand until they should be sent for. And, furthermore, he had been considerably surprised to hear himself mentioned by name by someone in authority who came to look for him in the shed amongst the prisoners, and who seemed vexed not to find him there, declaring that he knew Tom was to be among the rioters that night, and that he had made sure of catching him at last.

'Indeed!' said Tom, as he told us of this, 'and I could hardly keep from laughing out, for all the fright as I was in, when I was hear the chap asking after me and so particular anxious about me, and me close over his head in the thatch all the time! But what was make him ask about me like that? And how was he know as I should be there? That is what do puzzle me clean.'

I was as much puzzled as Tom was. The only thing I could

suggest was, that if we had been betrayed as we suspected, the traitor had had a special spite against Tom, and so had made special mention of him. Then he went on again with his story. He had recognised the voice of Rees Hughes amongst the prisoners in the shed, and was afraid that he was hurt rather badly. Tom had stayed on his perch till the police and soldiers were safely out of the way, and had then come over to see Martha and tell her what he had made up his mind to do.

He was thoroughly convinced that there was no safety for him in England any longer, and he meant to try and escape to America, and then send to Martha to come out to him there and marry him.

It was then my turn to tell my story of how I had shot a man, and had left my gun behind me marked with my name, so that I, too, must fly for my life. Tom's plan of getting to America seemed to me a very good one, and I said I thought I would go with him, and that then father and mother and Martha and the rest of the family had better come and join us as soon as we should be settled there. Tom was delighted to have me as a companion, and we hastily prepared for a start, there being no time to lose in getting away from where we were. We did not want to have more to carry than could be helped; but at the same time we did not want to have to show ourselves in shops as long as we were in a part of the country where there was a chance of our being known. So we settled to take enough food to keep us from the necessity of buying any just at first, and also as much money as could be spared for us.

In the midst of helping mother get together what was wanted, Martha, who had been very silent and seeming to be thinking deeply about something for some time, said suddenly:

'Was Pugh Morgan know of what you was mean to do last night? And was he know as Tom was mean to be with you?'

'Yes, of course,' answered I; 'Pugh do have known all about it from the first.'

'Well, was he help Rebecca too, then, himself?' continued Martha.

'Yes, indeed,' said I; 'though I was not see him nowhere last night neither – was you see anything of him, Tom?'

'Well, no,' returned Tom after considering the matter a minute; 'I was not see him as I was know of last night. But, there – 'tis not possible to see everyone in a crowd like that! Why was you want so much to know about he, all of a sudden, Martha?'

'Well, for this,' answered she; 'it do have come into my mind as it was no other than he as was bring the police upon Rebecca and was tell them to look out for Tom!'

Tom was taken aback at the idea. 'Pugh Morgan!' cried he, 'why, whatever shall make you think such a thing of him, Martha? Look, see! I never done nothing to hurt he in my life – and what for shall he want to hurt me like that?'

In answer, Martha told Tom of Pugh's love for her, and of the furious passion he had been in on the morning before, when she had told him plainly she would never marry him, and of how jealous he was of Tom, and how he had vowed vengeance against both her and Tom. Then I said how we had noticed that Pugh had not started with us the night before as he had said he should do, and how one of the men had fancied he had seen Pugh going towards Swansea. And when it all came to be put together there certainly did seem to be a good deal against Pugh. But I doubt that it would ever have occurred to me to think this if Martha had not put it into my head. There's no denying that a woman is wonderfully sharp about anything that concerns her young man!

Having sworn to do all I could to find out and punish whoever had betrayed us, and it being impossible for me to stay and see to it myself, I told Martha to tell Jenkin Thomas of our suspicions, and that he would know what to do. Though I saw no chance of taking part in bringing the traitor to judgment myself, yet I had the satisfaction of knowing that I left plenty behind me who would leave no stone unturned to discover him, and who would be very certain to pay him as he deserved.

As soon as our hasty preparations were completed, Tom and I said good-bye to mother and Martha and started on our flight. We had not yet made up our minds where to go at first, but we left Upper Killay walking openly along the road to Swansea, so that any of the neighbours who might be asked about us might say we had gone that way. A little way down that road was Bill Jones, watching to give notice of the approach of any enemies. And then we had to say good-bye to him also, and to tell him that he need watch no longer on our account.

Poor Bill! He cared for both of us after his own quiet fashion, and he was nearly as sad as I was at our having to part. When I told him that we meant to try and get to America, he declared that he should go there too, directly he should hear where I was there. And the last thing I did was to give him a message for me which was very near my heart, and which he promised faithfully to deliver. I told him to go to Penfawr and to see Miss Gwenllian herself, and to speak to her about me, and to tell her why I had been forced to go away. And I told him he must mind and explain to her what a cruel wrong and injustice Rebecca was fighting against, so that she might not think badly of me for what I had done. For I thought it was very likely that the people amongst whom she lived might not tell her of what was really being done – of how the magistrates were trying to support what was wrong and unfair, and to crush down those who only wanted justice – and that thus, for want of understanding how the matter really stood, she might condemn us as mere noisy, discontented, unmanageable rioters who had neither right nor reason on our side. So, for fear of this, I told Bill he must be sure to explain to her what our grievances were.

'And then, Bill,' I added, 'you must tell her as I was never forget her, and as I never shall forget her; and that ever since she was go away I was do what she was tell me as best I was know how to do it. And if she shall speak kindly of me, Bill, and shall seem to like to hear about me, tell her, you, how proud it was make me if she was ever give a thought to me – the poor boy as she was good to so long ago. Tell her as I was know of no way to pay her for her goodness but just by doing the things she would like me to do, and that she may be sure as I was always try to do that! And tell her, too, as I shall always keep the thought of her in my mind – whether ever I shall see her again or not – as what has been and is the best and dearest and most precious thing in my life – wherever I shall go and whatever shall happen to me.'

Perhaps you may think it odd that I should have said this when I had just gone right against all Miss Gwenllian's teaching by killing a man. But it did not seem strange to me, for I felt so sure of the righteousness of the cause for which I had been fighting that I thought no more of the man's death than a soldier does of anyone whom he may chance to kill in battle.

And so Tom and I took leave of Bill, and we departed from Killay – never to see it again.

CHAPTER XIII

As soon as we were out of sight of houses and people we turned off to the right, so as to leave the road, and buried ourself deeply in Clyne Wood, where we could venture to stop and settle more definitely what we had better do. For though we had made up our minds to try and reach America, yet how that was to be accomplished we had but very little idea, except that people sailed from Liverpool to get there. Anyhow our first proceeding must be to get away from our own neighbourhood where people would know us, and it occurred to us that we should do this most easily by getting taken on board a vessel if we could manage it. Vessels often sailed from the Mumbles and from Oxwich to various places, and if we could join one of these vessels we did not mind much where it would land us, so long as it was somewhere where no one would know us; and we thought that one place would be as good as another for getting from to America.

Having settled this much, the next question was, whether the Mumbles or Oxwich would be the best place to take the ship at – the Mumbles being within two or three miles of us and Oxwich being about nine miles off. But though the Mumbles was the nearest, yet it was also much nearer Swansea than the other, and so we determined to try for a vessel at Oxwich, where there would be less chance of our enemies being on the look-out for us; and we also resolved that we would keep hidden by day and only travel at night, so as, if possible, to avoid being seen by anyone. Of course we could not tell whether the search after me had begun yet or not; but we knew it was sure to begin as soon as my gun should be picked up, and we meant to take all precautions. We did not leave Clyne Wood, where we could keep ourselves hidden, till it was dark; but from the edge of the wood we were rather alarmed to see a couple of policemen crossing Clyne Common towards Fairwood in the direction that we meant to have taken. This might or might not have anything to do with us; but at all events the sight of them made us uneasy, and we consequently determined to give them a wide berth and go to Oxwich by the longest way – round by Carter's Ford and then across Cefn Bryn – instead of going the shortest way by Park and Penmaen.

As soon as it was night we left our hiding-place and crossed Fairwood by Carter's Ford and reached a farm named Killibion, which is on the north side of the hill called Cefn Bryn; as Oxwich Bay is two or three miles on the south side of this hill, we had now only to cross the long ridge and descend into the bay, where we hoped to find a vessel. But the darkness was now changing to daylight, and so we took possession of an old shed that we found near Killibion, in which we rested safely during the day, making sure that we should easily get down to Oxwich in the course of the next night. Our food was disappearing rather faster than we liked, but still we had enough left to keep us from having to buy any for the present.

The day's rest refreshed us both greatly; and when it was dark we set out to cross the Cefn Bryn ridge without any misgivings as to our reaching the sea easily before daylight; for though neither of us had ever been there before, yet we knew that the distance we had to go was so short, that we thought, even if we did not take the straightest way, we should still have plenty of time to make our way to Oxwich after we should have got across the hill.

When we left the shed there was a light rain falling, which, however, we did not mind much, as a moonlight night is never as dark as one when there is no moon, even though there may be clouds which hide her from sight. But mist is worse than cloud or rain, and by the time we were halfway up Cefn Bryn a thick mist came on in which it was impossible to see a yard before one, and which completely puzzled us. On we went, however, with nothing to guide us except the knowledge that we ought to keep going up hill continually until we should get to the top. But the hillside was covered with great pieces of rock, which often made it difficult to know with any certainty whether we were going up hill or down. Streams and small bogs abounded also, and we remembered having been told that on Cefn Bryn were one or two deep bogs which anyone who got into would have a difficulty in getting out of again. We heard the water gurgling and bubbling around us, and felt the soft ground shake and quake under our footsteps when we passed over the wettest parts; but whereabouts we were we had no idea as we floundered and struggled on at random in the intense darkness.

All of a sudden, Tom, who was close to me though I could not see him, called out; and at the same moment there was a great splash.

'What is it, Tom?' cried I. But no answer did I have, nor did I hear any further sound. I stretched out my arms to try and feel him, but in vain. Then it struck me that he must have fallen into one of the small deep pools that are often to be found in boggy places. I was horrified at the thought, for I knew he could not swim a stroke; and how was I to help him when I could not see a yard before my nose, and could not tell whether he was in front of me or on either side? I again called out his name, in hopes he might be able to hear me and make some sound to guide me to him; but I got no answer – I could hear nothing except the moaning of the wind and the trickling of water; and there, most likely, the poor fellow was drowning close to me, while I, a good swimmer, was doing nothing to save him. Oh, it was horrible! – more horrible than anyone can fancy unless he has been in such a situation himself!

Then I made a step nearer to the direction in which I fancied I had heard the splash, and lay down on the ground and began feeling for the pool. It was very near me, and just as I stooped over it and felt the water with my hands, I heard a very faint sort of gasp close on one side of me. I made a frantic grab towards the sound; and if ever any man was glad in this world, that man was me at that moment when I felt my hand strike against hair! Tom had risen to the top for an instant, and was just sinking again when I touched him, so that it was the merest shave I did not miss him altogether. But a miss is as good as a mile, and as it was I had safe hold of him, and in another minute or so I had pulled him out of the pool and had him lying safely beside me on the rushes. Though I could not see him for the darkness, yet I could feel him; and to touch him, and know my companion was safe, was quite enough to make me perfectly happy after the terror of the last few minutes. All my troubles and dangers were forgotten in the joy of his safety, and I laughed out loud in my delight. It was not only that I was fond of Tom and looked on him as my future brother-in-law; but also, when I thought I had lost him, I seemed to be seized with a dread of the utter loneliness that would have come to me if I should lose the companion of my flight and exile – the only person to whom I could speak freely, and from whom I need to have no secrets.

Tom soon came to himself again, and was none the worse for the adventure, except that he was wet through and through. Unluckily he had been carrying almost all the food we had left, and this had fallen out of his pocket and got lost in the water, so that one small slice of bread and meat was all that now remained to us.

We went on with the greatest care for a short time after

this; but then, getting hopelessly bewildered in the mist, we thought we had better give up the idea of going on till we should be able to see something of where we were, so we sat down shivering in our wet things, and waited for the mist to clear away. This did not happen till long after dawn, and we had then still some distance to go before we reached the top of the hill.

From here we looked own upon the sea, and saw the village of Oxwich about four miles off beneath us. It was Saturday – market-day – and as the morning was far advanced and more people than usual would be about, we were afraid to go straight down to our destination, and thought it would be more prudent to put off getting there for another day and pass that day in hiding somewhere, it being our great object that no one at all should see us till we got on board a ship, so that our enemies should have no means of tracking our course, and no clue whatever as to what direction we had taken. On the bare side of Cefn Bryn, however, no shelter at all was to be had, so we made our way down as fast as we could to the old castle of Penrice, whose ruined walls offered a good hiding-place. It was very distasteful to us thus to have to spend another day in inaction; for the anxiety and suspense we were in made the day seem very long when it had to be passed in doing nothing instead of hurrying on our escape. We were in a state of considerable bodily discomfort also, for . we were very hungry, having soon finished the last small piece of food we had left, and were wet besides. Unluckily the sun was behind the clouds all day, or it might have dried and warmed us; so we had to get through the day as best we could behind the old castle walls, wet, cold, hungry, and anxious – speculating on whether my gun had yet been found, what our enemies were doing, and whether we should succeed in finding a vessel to take us off at once when we reached the sea.

And what had I done, thought I, that I should be thus outcast from my home and friends – forced to fly for my life and tremble at the idea of being seen? I had done nothing to be ashamed of – nothing but what I gloried in having done! My troubles had come upon me merely because I had dared to lift my hand against wrong and injustice! If that was how I was to be treated in England, then indeed it was better to seek a home elsewhere – in America or any other land where every man (as I had heard) was listened to alike, and had a voice in making the laws which he was expected to obey.

Bitter thoughts like these filled my mind during that long day whilst I shivered and longed for warmth, and food, and comfort as I lay on the damp grass at Penrice. We slept a little during part of the day, but were too uncomfortable to sleep long. It served to amuse us now and then to look out through the chinks of the castle walls at the modern house just below, and to watch the inhabitants going in and out of the house, without over dreaming how near they were to two of Rebecca's children!

Everything, however, comes to an end in time, and so at last that weary day finished, and in the dark we crossed the marsh and reached Oxwich Bay. We were now obliged to hold some communication with our fellow-men, both in order to make inquiries about a vessel and also to procure some food, we being ravenously hungry. There was no need for both of us to show ourselves, however, so Tom remained out of sight amongst the numerous sandbanks which surround the bay, whilst I strolled into the village as soon as the inhabitants were stirring. I put on as careless an air as I could and entered into conversation with the first man I met, asking him when any vessels were likely to be in, as I was not a little disappointed to see none there at that moment. He informed me that vessels hardly ever stayed for more than one tide in Oxwich, as it was an unsafe anchorage, and that no ship was expected again there for several days to come. This was a bad hearing for me, for we certainly could not venture to wait as long as that, and what made matters still more provoking was that the man said there had been a schooner loading with limestone for Devonshire only the day before, and that her captain had been inquiring about extra hands, so that we might have got off without delay, and have been already in a place of comparative safety, if only we had not got lost in the mist on Cefn Bryn, and thus delayed our arrival at Oxwich by twenty-four hours! There was now, however, nothing for it but to try and account for my being there by saying I was a stranger in search of work, and that I wanted to find out where I could buy something to eat. But the people to whom I spoke seemed to wonder at me for wanting to purchase food on a Sunday morning at that early hour, and I fancied they did not look much as if they believed my story, and I thought the sooner we got away from there the better.

When I returned to Tom and told him the unsatisfactory result of my inquiries, his face fell considerably.

'We do have wasted a lot of time in coming here for nothing then,' he remarked, 'and our only chance to get off by sea shall be to go back to the Mumbles – and the Mumbles do be a sight nearer Swansea than be safe. But I do suppose as us must go and try there now, Evan – eh?'

'That's what I do think myself,' I replied; 'and I do think, too, as us ought to keep right along the coast to go there, where there be nothing but sheep and birds to see us, and not go a step farther inland nor we can help.'

'Shall us wait here to today, or go on at once?' said Tom; 'these here sandbanks was not high enough to be a very first-rate hiding-place, and they be very near to the village too.'

'Oh, 'tis best to go away from here now soon, I think,' answered I; 'us can wait till everyone shall be gone to church or chapel, and there shall be no one about to see us cross the sands. And us can eat a bit of vittles meanwhile – look, see what I do have got!'

With that I displayed the food I had bought, and we readily set to work and made a hearty meal. It was a beautiful hot day, and when we had breakfasted we lay contentedly enjoying the sunshine till the stopping of the Oxwich church-bell, which had been ringing for service, warned us to get up and continue our journey whilst the coast was likely to be clear. Turning back towards the east we left Oxwich and reached Three Cliffs Bay. Here we were disgusted to find a couple of pleasure-parties come down to picnic and spend the day at the sea. Of course we might have crossed the bay openly in spite of them; but we had such a nervous horror of being seen by anyone who might put our foes on our scent, that we preferred to stay concealed amongst the rocks at the west end of the bay till they should go out of sight.

'Silly idiots!' muttered Tom; 'was there no place but this as would suit them for to eat their dinners or teas at? Why they have plenty of sea and sand too, just close to Swansea; why was not that do for them instead of coming all these miles down here?'

'Well, so one would think,' observed I; 'but maybe they was like to have rocks to sit upon, and there do not be no rocks near Swansea.'

'Rocks indeed!' returned Tom angrily; 'they do have bathing-machines though, and the steps of them be quite so good as rocks to sit on, and drier too! And then they could get into the machine for cover if it do come to rain. It was a deal better for they to stay at home and not come hindering us like this.'

The pleasure-parties got out of our way at last; but they had delayed us so long that we thought we had no chance of finding any vessels sailing from the Mumbles that night, and that we had better not get there till the next morning; then we hoped we should get off to sea at once and avoid any waiting about in such an extremely dangerous neighbourhood. Consequently, soon after we had crossed Three Cliffs Bay, we began looking out for some cave in which to pass the night, for I had heard that there were several big caves along the rocks at that part of the coast, and unless we found a cave we had no chance of shelter without leaving the edge of the sea and going inland, where we should be sure to meet people.

After hunting along the cliffs for some time, and peering into every chink and cranny, Tom, who was a little below me, said he had found a hole, but that it was too small for anyone to walk in at, and that the entrance was almost choked up with stones. I was very tired of scrambling over the sharp-pointed rocks in the hot sun, and I clambered down to see what he had found, hoping it might turn out to be the mouth of one of the caves of which I had heard.

I found him standing in a crevice between two rocks which was heaped up with shingle; and at the end of the crevice was a small hole into the rock just large enough to admit a man's body, and the cliff rose steep and straight far above the hole.

'Us shall see what it do be like, anyhow,' said I; and, lying down on the rough shingle, I managed, by crawling on my hands and knees, and wriggling on my stomach, to get myself into the hole, though not without considerable difficulty. At first my eyes were too much dazzled by the sudden change from light to dark to see anything, but I could feel that there was room all round me, and gradually raising myself very cautiously so as not to hit my head against the roof, I stood upright. Then I called Tom to come in, and as my eyes became used to the darkness I could see something of the sort of place we had got into. It was a cave big enough to have held twenty men or more upon its floor, and it seemed to run up to an immense height, but how far it extended upwards we could not tell on account of the dim light. The rocky sides were wet and shining, and there was a slow mournful dripping of water into a large pool in the middle of the cave.

'Well, I suppose as it shall do for us tonight,' said Tom, 'but it do be a mighty damp unwholesome sort of place to my mind!'

It certainly was not a very tempting place of abode, though convenient to us just then, and as it was far pleasanter outside in the sun than inside in the damp gloomy cavern, we crawled out again in the open air, and seated ourselves within easy reach of our hiding-place, so as to be able to get back to it on any alarm.

Judging by the light, I should think it must have been about seven or eight o'clock in the evening when I fell into a doze, and was dreaming a pleasant restful dream about Miss Gwenllian, and home, and Martha, and the rest, when I was suddenly touched by Tom, who at the same time laid his hand on my mouth for fear I might speak or make a noise. In my sleep I had been happy and contented and free from all care, and the sudden arousing from my dream made the realities of my life of danger, discomfort, and restless anxiety seem bitterer than ever.

'There do be some people about somewhere overhead of us,' whispered Tom; 'I was not see no one, but I was hear voices. It do be best to get back to hiding, I do think.'

The distance from the cave was very short, and we crawled cautiously back to it, keeping under every projecting piece of rock which could conceal us from whoever might be the speakers on the cliff above us.

'Was you think they was looking for me, Tom?' asked I in a low voice when we had regained our shelter.

'I was not know no more than you,' replied he; 'I was not hear a word as they was say, only it be safest to be out of sight when there be people about. 'Tis lucky for us now as it be all little stones outside the cave; if so be as it was sand, anyone could see the footmarks of us coming in here.'

When our eyes had again got used to the dim light we examined the sides of the cave, and saw that, in case of visitors coming in, it would be easy for us to scramble some way up the sides to keep out of their way.

Before long the voices came nearer and nearer, till they were close outside our hiding-place and we could hear what they said.

We soon made out that the speakers were a party of police who were in search of me; but they seemed to be somewhat tired, and very doubtful as to whether they were going in the most likely direction to find me.

'Well, for my part I don't believe as he be anywhere, hereabouts,' said one sulky-sounding voice. 'You see he left Oxwich at eleven or twelve o'clock; well, it stands to reason as he must have got miles farther than this by now. Besides, how do we know as he ever came this way at all? Why shouldn't he have gone inland just as likely as to be sticking to the sea-coast?'

'Why, you see,' answered another voice, 'all as we has to go upon is that he wanted to get took into a ship, and a man as wants that isn't very likely to go inland anyhow.'

'The fellow at Oxwich as told us about him,' observed a third voice, 'thought he seen two men crossing the bay.'

'And that's one thing makes me doubt whether the party as we heard on at Oxwich is the same party as we wants,' said the first voice; 'I calls it folly to be grinding along on a wild-goose chase like this, and I votes as we either goes somewhere else, or else just goes back and says as how we can't find him.'

'Why, here's a queer little hole!' exclaimed some other voice which sounded very close outside the cave; 'what if he should have hidden himself in here?'

Then came a discussion as to whether I was likely to be in

there or not, none of the party seeming very willing to go in himself, and each one urging the other to go; and at last one man, after considerable pressure from his comrades, said he didn't mind giving a look in to see what was there; an announcement which made Tom and me retreat a little way up the side.

A great deal of commotion and scuffling about in the stones outside ensued, and presently the head, neck, and shoulders of a man made their appearance within the mouth of the cave. We having been for sometime in the darkness, could see him pretty well, but he, having just come in from the daylight could see nothing whatever.

'Dark as pitch in here!' cried he, without attempting to bring in the rest of his body; ''tis no use at all to try and look in here without lights. And a nasty damp hole it feels like, full of toads and snakes, I expect! And I've rubbed half my skin off in getting in, I believe; no man in his senses would come in here for choice, I'm sure. I'm not going any farther in without lights, I can tell you!'

And he slowly wriggled himself backwards till he got out again. He moved so slowly, and made such absurd puffing and wheezing noises in getting in and out of the hole, that we felt sure he must be rather stout and could not have at all enjoyed the narrow entrance to our retreat.

The voices went on talking outside for awhile, and finally the speakers concluded that it was not likely to be any good searching the cave, and that they certainly could not attempt it without lights, and that they were very tired and meant to do no more that night, and so that they should go home. And then we heard their voices gradually dying away in the distance as they departed and left us to enjoy peace and safety for at least a few hours longer.

CHAPTER XIV

After a few hours of such broken sleep as we could get on the rocky floor of the cave, we left its shelter and crossed Caswell Bay and Langland Bay, reaching the Mumbles Hill soon after dawn. There was no use in descending into the village at once, so we sat down for awhile on the top of the hill, and watched the light broadening over the sea as the rising sun touched the vessels in the harbour one by one and glistened on their dewy masts and decks. The tide runs out nearly a mile at the Mumbles, and it was then dead low water, so that the little fleet of oyster-dredging smacks, or 'skiffs' as they are always called, lay high and dry on the sands at about a quarter or half a mile between the village and the far-off tide. As we sat looking at all these skiffs, the sight of them inspired Tom with a fresh idea.

'Look you now,' said he, 'even if us do get taken on board some one of them big ships, it is a chance that she shall be going to start just that very minute. Very likely as she shall wait some hours, or maybe the whole day, first; and if so, and if the police do come here after us, then there shall be an end of our going with her whatever. But I do think us can do better than that. What if us was to hire one of them oyster-dredger boats for a day's sail? So soon as we do be safe away from land us can pretend to change our minds and say as us do want to go to Devonshire and get the boatmen to take us there. And then no one shall know where us shall have landed, not until the boatmen shall get back again here.'

I highly applauded this suggestion, even though it would make a big hole in our small stock of money; for now that we knew for certain that enemies were so close on our track, it was evident that if we did not get away at once we should probably not do so at all. We had just got up to climb down the hill into the village when two magpies flew past us and perched upon a dead tree some little distance off. Tom stopped short at seeing them, and looked quite frightened.

'Look, see there, Evan!' he exclaimed, pointing to the two birds.

'Well, I don't see nothing but a couple of 'pies,' replied I; 'what of them?'

'Was you not know as two 'pies do always mean trouble to whoever do see them?' answered he; 'them birds do be telling us of trouble to come for sure!'

'Nonsense, man!' cried I, laughing, for I did not believe in such things myself; 'them two birds be only going to suck some eggs or do some mischief somewhere or other – but that is all the trouble as they do tell about! They was chance to fly this way, but 'tis folly for to think as they do know anything about us or what be going to happen to us. Indeed and I do think as us have enough of real dangers to be afraid of without wanting to go frightening ourselves for a couple of harmless birds into the bargain!'

But Tom was not to be laughed out of his superstition; he seemed to have quite lost his spirits and courage; was as down-cast as if the prison-doors were already opening to shut us in; and declared that some terrible misfortune was certainly coming upon either one or both of us.

It was about five o'clock when we reached the Mumbles village, where a few people were now beginning to be about. A man in a rough, sailorlike-looking dress, was standing in the road and looking out to sea with a telescope, and to him we went, saying that we had a mind to take a boat for the day, and asking him if he could direct us to anyone who had a skiff for hire. The man eyed our travel-stained clothes and untidy appearance with a look of considerable contempt, and then said:

'Well, you two are about the rummiest-looking pair as ever I saw to want a skiff for going pleasuring in! 'Tain't such as you that hire a boat for a day's sail in general. You can't do that without money, my fine fellows, and you don't look to have too much of that between the two of you.'

'Ay, but us may have it for all that, maybe,' returned Tom angrily. 'What do hinder us two honest working men as have got a holiday and a few pounds to spend from wanting to do the same as a gentleman for once? Our money do be so good as his, I do suppose? Look, see, what shall you call that?' Saying this, Tom pulled out the purse which held our money and tossed it up into the air, and then went on: 'Never you trouble yourself with what be no business of yours, my man, but just give a civil answer to a civil question, and tell if you do know where us shall be able to hire a boat.'

The man became civil when he saw the money, and said he had not meant to offend us, and that as he owned a skiff himself we could have that one if we liked. We soon came to terms, being in too much hurry to be off to stay bargaining, and readily agreeing to pay what he asked. Then I asked him what he thought of the weather, and whether the wind would suit for sailing towards the opposite coast.

'If the wind should hold as it be now,' replied he, looking up at the sky, 'it'll suit best for running up the Channel past Swansea and towards Neath way; but it don't look over and above settled to my mind, and I wouldn't wonder if it was to come on rather rough for pleasuring by-and-by. Be you pretty good sailors?'

'Oh, never you trouble your head about that!' answered I. 'We do be good sailors enough, and it don't make no odds to we what the weather was be. But us do want to go now at once, and not be wasting our holiday on shore here.'

'Well, well,' returned the man, 'we shall start so soon as 'tis possible; but 'tis no use for you to be in a hurry till the tide shall have run in far enough to float the skiff – look, there she be with the others high and dry on the sand, and there she must be till the sea reaches her. I shall go and look up my mate to come with us, and maybe the water will be almost up to her by the time we are ready.' So saying he walked off to fetch his mate, leaving Tom and me to pace up and down the road in a fever of impatience as we watched the slow advance of the rising tide towards the skiffs. Slowly and gradually the water crept over the sand; and we thought that surely no tide had ever before taken so long to rise! Our anxiety and impatience was increased by Tom's discovering that he had left his neck-handkerchief in the cave where we spent the night, so that if our enemies should go there with lights, as they had talked of doing, they would find this sign of our recent present there, and would be all the keener in their pursuit.

When our boatman and his mate returned, we said we should go down to the skiff at once, and wait in her until she should be afloat; so we all four went and established ourselves in her, and the two men began preparing the sails and everything else, so that we might have no delay in getting off when once the water should be high enough. Once on board we felt a little more easy. The ripples of water had at last touched our skiff and were beginning to surround her; and we alternately watched their progress, and cast anxious looks towards the land, where we feared at every moment to see our foes appear in search of us. Suddenly I saw the figures of five or six men make their appearance on the brow of the hill which we had crossed a few hours before. That they were police I had very little doubt, though it was too far off to make them out clearly. Still – we were not lost yet; for it was some distance down from the top of the hill to the village; and they would be sure to stop and search the hillside as they came; and then it was more than a quarter of a mile across the sands from the village to our skiff.

Small waves were dashing already against the side of the boat and spreading farther and farther over the sand around.

'We'll be afloat now just,' observed the boatman, who had been busy about the sails and tackle and did not notice those figures descending the hill whose motions were of such absorbing interest to Tom and me. Then, turning to his companion, he exclaimed: 'Why, Jack! Where be them sweeps as I told you to bring down? You never went and left them at the house, now, did you?'

'Do b'lieve but I did though!' replied Jack; 'I'll step up after 'em and have 'em down now directly.'

Tom and I were almost out of our senses with vexation to hear this. What the sweeps might be we had not the slightest idea, but waiting for them to be fetched from the house might be our ruin.

'It's pity to lose so much time,' said I, speaking as calmly as I could; 'can't us do without them?'

'No, no,' returned the man; 'I won't go without 'em, or else where would we be if it should fall calm? Not that I see any chance of that happening today – but still, I must have 'em. Jack'll have 'em down in a jiffy. Run you, Jack, quick!'

So Jack ran off after the sweeps, whilst we had to sit quietly in the boat and watch the proceedings of our pursuers. I heard Tom mutter to himself: 'They magpies knew it – I was know it of them all along!' But except for that we were perfectly silent, for our anxiety was too intense for speaking.

Our foes got to the bottom of the hill and entered the village just as a decided heave of the skiff told us she was at last afloat. At that moment Jack was just getting on board of us with the long oars which they call sweeps.

The police would be sure speedily to hear of us from some of the many idlers who always lounge about a place ready to mind everyone's business except their own; and that they would have no difficulty in knowing where we were and coming straight across the sand to us, because the oyster-dredging season had not yet begun, so that our skiff was the only one that was not lying idle, and the men on board of her and her readiness to start were unmistakable evidences of our presence. A strong gusty wind was blowing, and this was in our favour, as it would prevent voices from being heard if they should shout after us.

Jack scrambled on board – our skiff was unmoored from the float that held her – the mainsail was unfurled – the skipper took the helm – and, with feelings of intense relief, we at last found ourselves slipping rapidly through the water, and threading our way first in and out of the other skiffs that were tossing at their moorings, and then amongst the numerous trading vessels that were anchored farther out in the harbour. Just as we reached the farthest out of these we could see people running down to the shore we had left waving their hands and making frantic signs.

'I wonder what be a-going on there?' observed our boatman, who happened to look back and see the commotion on shore.

'Can't say, I'm sure,' replied Jack. 'They was all quiet enough when I was up after the sweeps. Maybe 'tis the captain of one of these here vessels as has spent the night on shore, and wants his boat sent off for him in a hurry, and has got a few other chaps to help him make a row.'

'Likely enough,' returned the skipper, carelessly; 'I daresay 'twill be the French brig's captain as came in on Friday – they French fellows do make such a fuss about everything! Look to the tops'le, Jack – we'll hoist it if so be there ain't too much wind.'

So the two men, to our great relief, occupied themselves with the skiff, and paid no further attention to what might be going on on shore. But it had been a narrow shave for us.

Another few minutes' difference in the tide would have seen us prisoners – and being taken meant being hung, for me, at all events.

The wind was fresh, and our boat was a fast one, and we cut through the water at a great rate. There was enough sea to make us roll considerably, but neither Tom nor I were ill; neither of us having ever been to sea before, it was just a chance whether we turned out good sailors or not, but luckily we were quite able to make good my boast that we did not mind what sort of weather we had.

Presently we began talking to the boatmen of different places we wanted to see, and then Tom pretended to be seized with a sudden wish to go and have a look at Devonshire. I made believe also that the idea was quite new to me, and exclaimed: 'Why not go now when us do have a couple of days' holiday? Couldn't us go there instead of anywhere else?' The skipper shook his head doubtfully. 'I suppose as we *might* manage it with tacking; but the wind be best to go on up Channel today. 'Tis looking very much like dirty weather coming on to my mind, and indeed I don't know but what we would be wiser to go back now soon to the Mumbles instead of thinking of going on farther.'

At this, however, Tom and I cried out in indignation; and we so insisted upon trying for Devonshire that at last the skipper gave way and changed our course accordingly, though not without many doubtful glances at the sky, and very evident reluctance.

We got on but slowly on our new course, and the weather grew worse as the day went on. The sky became wholly overcast; the strong, gusty wind came in more and more frequent puffs, and brought scuds of rain also once or twice. The two sailors looked uneasy, and said something about the wisdom of going back if possible; but Tom and I pretended to think nothing of the bad weather, laughing at them for minding it, and promising them extra pay if they kept on, and did not balk us of our holiday excursion. The skipper said that if we persisted in trying to reach Devonshire we should probably have to be out in the Channel all night; but we replied we were not afraid of that, and, what with our persuasions and promises, we overcame his objections and induced him to keep on the former course in spite of the threatening bank of black clouds that was gathering heavily to windward. The wind and rain increased, and before long we were surrounded by thick driving rain, which made it impossible to see objects at a couple of hundred yards off. Matters began to get serious, and the two sailors held hasty consultations together and seemed to have very little idea of where abouts we were. They changed our course several times in a very undecided manner. At last, as the darkness of night came on in addition to the darkness of the storm, and as the weather seemed to be getting continually worse, the skipper told us fairly that he really had no idea of where we were, except that we must be somewhere or other in the Bristol Channel; but that he did not think that mattered much, as he did not expect the skiff could live much longer in such a storm, and he believed we should all go to the bottom before very many more hours should have passed if the sea should continue to get wilder, as it was then doing.

When Tom heard this he looked at me and said: 'Remember them magpies, Evan; *they* knew it.'

But that was all we said, for the noise and rush of the water and the creaking of the planks made speaking a difficult matter. We were so tossed about that we could not stand alone, but had to cling tightly to the rail lest we should be washed overboard by the great waves that dashed like sledge-hammers against our skiff, pouring in torrents over the deck and back again into the sea under the rail. Tom and I, being quite strange to this sort of thing, were made dizzy by the violent pitching up and down of the boat, and the incessant roaring thunder of the sea and wind; and all four of us made up our minds that we should very soon be drowned. For my part this expectation did not at all make me regret having set out on the voyage, for, whatever the end of it might be, I was at all events better off than if I had stayed on shore. Had I done that I must have been taken, and if taken I should be hanged, so that to me it was a choice of deaths; and I decidedly preferred being drowned to dying by the hands of my enemies and letting them have the satisfaction of getting rid of me.

For a time that seemed almost endless we tossed and struggled on in the rain and waves and darkness; and then at last the end came. The skiff was driven upon a sandy beach, the sea broke furiously over her directly she struck, and I found myself washed overboard into the foaming, raging waves, which gave me no chance of helping myself by swimming, but dashed me along like a cork, and flung me upon the shore without my having the smallest power of resisting them. The instant I touched the land I made one great effort, and succeeded in getting out of reach of the sea before it could return and sweep me back again. Thus it came to pass that I unexpectedly found myself safe and sound on dry land almost before I had had time to know how I got there.

When I had collected my senses a little I tried to shout out loud, in hopes of getting an answer from Tom or the boatmen; but the roaring of the sea and wind completely drowned my voice, and I found I must wait for daylight before I should have any chance of knowing what had become of my companions. The storm subsided as day began to dawn. At first I could see nothing but open sea before me and high sand-banks behind; but as the light grew clearer I made out the figure of a man nearly a mile off along the sands, and on going towards him I was delighted to find that it was none other than Tom, who had been cast upon the beach in the same way that I had, and had afterwards moved some distance off in the darkness without knowing where he was going.

We saw nothing whatever of the two boatmen, and we had not the very least idea of where we were – we might be in England or in Wales, or on Lundy Island for all we could tell. However, our shipwreck seemed to us very much in our favour, for thus we had escaped from our own neighbourhood and had left absolutely no trace at all by which we could be followed.

'You see as they two old magpies was mean no harm to us after all!' said I, laughing. 'We did seem like going to have bad luck last night, but now it do have turned to good luck for us.'

But Tom only looked serious when I mentioned the magpies and answered: "Tis wrong you do be to be laughing at them. There be many as says that two 'pies do bring trouble to them that do see them. And if that was not true, why was the people say it?'

CHAPTER XV

As the daylight grew brighter and we looked around us, we could see only two things – sand and sea; nothing else was in sight, and we saw not a vestige of our boatmen. Either they had been drowned, or else they must have left the shore in the night; so we thought no more about them, and began walking away from the sea over the sand-banks, hoping soon to meet with someone to tell us what part of the country we were in.

The extent of those sand-banks was wonderful, and we thought we should never get to the end of them. As fast as we reached the top of one sand-hill, we saw another and another before us and on all sides of us; and they were all so much alike that we soon got quite confused as to which way was the sea and which way was the land likely to be, and several times came to places which we were quite sure we had passed over before, so that we became disheartened, thinking that we were walking round and round in a circle. Altogether we were not in a very cheerful condition; for our clothes were wet through; we were in want of food; we had had no sleep for one night, and very little the night before; and the deep sand was very heavy and tiring to walk over. No living things did we see amongst those weary sand-hills, except rabbits, of which there were plenty; but, however acceptable they would have been to us as breakfast, they were of no use when we had no means of catching or cooking them. Seeing such a lot of them about put me in mind of the first time ever I had gone to Penfawr, when Squire Tudor had found his rabbit in my pocket, and I made Tom laugh by telling him about it. After long wandering we at last got away from that hateful sand, and had the satisfaction of again treading on firm ground, that did not let one sink in over the ankles at every step. We soon came to a road, and had not gone far along it before we met with a boy, from whom we ascertained that we were about three or four miles from Bridgend, and who told us the way to get to that town.

It was a great thing to know exactly where we were, and when we separated from the boy, we again considered our situation and prospects, and discussed what was best to do in the altered circumstances.

Our Devonshire scheme was of course at an end now. But we had heard of wild mountains existing in the country somewhere not far from Bridgend; and we determined to try and reach these mountains, where we might manage to exist without attracting observation, until we should find means of making our way to Liverpool and thence to America. We were safe for the present from any immediate pursuit, as our enemies knew nothing of us, except that we had left the Mumbles in a skiff; and if the wreck of the skiff should become known, it would very likely be supposed that we were drowned. Therefore our shipwreck seemed to be a very great advantage to us, and had secured for us at least that most important article – time.

Our first object was to get something to eat and drink, and then to find out which road to take to reach the mountains; so we proceeded to Bridgend and entered a public-house, and called for food. There was hardly anyone there except the landlord, at first; but by the time we had almost finished our meal, a good many more men had dropped into the inn kitchen and ordered bread and cheese and beer, it being then the fashionable hour for lunch at Bridgend.

As for Tom and me, what with our shipwreck, and our sleepless nights, and our long tramp over the heavy sand,

and one thing and another, we had been a good deal done up when we got to the inn, and were now thoroughly satisfied to sit quiet and rest ourselves, dawdling over the last of our breakfast, and picking up the information we wanted as to the way to the mountains, from some of the men who came in to lunch. Most of these asked where Griffiths was as they came in, and seemed surprised that he had not yet come; and presently I got curious to know who he was, and asked one of the men about him. I was told that Griffiths was a great scholar, who could read and write quite beautifully; and that he generally came into the public-house at that time of day, to read or write letters for any person of inferior education who might require his services and be willing to pay for them. The reason why he was expected with so much interest today was that it was Tuesday – on which day the weekly newspaper, called *The Bridgend Budget*, came out – and it was Griffiths's custom to come and read this paper at the inn, and to impart the most interesting bits of news to the rest of the inn company, unless anyone should be rash enough to put him out of temper, in which case not one word could he be got to utter.

Just after I had received this information the great man himself made his appearance, and was received with the utmost deference and respect by all, from the landlord down. Griffiths carried *The Bridgend Budget* in his hand, and after a few careless words with the landlord and one or two other men whom he honoured with his notice, he seated himself in the most comfortable chair, called for a glass of beer, lit his pipe, settled his spectacles across his nose, and proceeded to unfold the paper, and read it to himself with much crackling and rustling of the leaves as he turned them over. His whole air showed that he was perfectly aware of the superiority given him by education, and he evidently considered that whatever respect and attentions might be paid him would be no more than his due. The other men left off talking, and

waited silently till he should see fit to give them the benefit
of his great learning and read them out the news. It was not
long before their patience was rewarded. He began slowly
reading aloud various bits of intelligence which he thought
interesting, making his own comments on them as he read:
'Meat gone up to fivepence a pound in Cardiff: I do call it
quite sinful to raise the price of meat like that – no poor man
shall be able to afford it at that rate. A gigantic gooseberry,
weighing two ounces, has been grown in the garden of Mr
Jones – well! That be a wonderful fine fruit, sure-ly! On
Thursday Her Majesty the Queen went for a ride in the park
– I've been told by one that had it from them as knew, that
she rides a deal.'

Here the reader slowly turned over a leaf of the paper and
went on reading the other side. 'Hullo! Here be big print!' he
exclaimed. 'What be all this about? "Rioting in the neighbourhood of Swansea" – to think of that! Oh, now I do see, it was
all along of that Rebecca as we have heard talk on.'

At this point Griffiths paused, refilled his pipe, sipped his
beer, and then continued his reading silently, evidently doing
this in order that his audience might press him to tell them
more of the choice bits of news he had discovered, and that
thus his importance might be increased. Nor was he disappointed in this expectation, being very soon petitioned by
the other men to let them hear 'what was to do about it,' a
thirst for intelligence which he graciously consented to gratify.

'Well, listen now then,' said he, stretching out his legs and
settling his spectacles afresh; 'here's enough of news for you
– indeed to goodness 'tis a mercy as we don't have no such
goings on here! All the account of it is copied into this paper
out of *The Swansea Swallow*, I see.'

Then he began reading a long account of the row at Pontardulais. Tom and I could have told them a good deal more
about it than the newspaper writer, who certainly could not

have been in the fight himself, nor yet have thoroughly understood what had been told him about it, judging by the deal of nonsense he wrote on the subject. But the Bridgend men took it all in as absolutely true, and we were much amused in listening to it all, without hearing anything that interested us particularly until the following bit was read out:

'One of the prisoners, named Rees Hughes, is so severely wounded that he has had to be moved into the hospital, and his recovery is thought doubtful. None of the police were killed. It is with the deepest regret that we announce that our old and much-respected neighbour, the Squire of Penfawr, was shot dead in the fracas. He had insisted on accompanying the party who went to suppress the rioters, and behaved with the utmost gallantry up to the moment when he fell. He dropped lifeless from his horse immediately on the shot striking him, and neither spoke nor moved again.'

My head swam and the room seemed to go round with me when I heard this. I tried to jump up – not quite knowing where I was nor what I was doing – but Tom, seeing something was amiss with me, managed to keep me down in my seat. He did not know exactly what was exciting me so suddenly; but he concluded that I was over-tired and somehow nervous, so that it upset me to hear of the man whom I had shot.

The truth was that my mind was all in a storm like the sea the night before; and that my wits and senses were, for the moment, as driven about, and tossed, and helpless as the skiff in which we had been wrecked.

To think that I – I who would have shot myself sooner than harm anyone belonging to Miss Gwenllian – that *I* should have been the one to shoot her father! That it should be *I* who had brought sorrow and trouble to the person whom I most cared for in the whole world! It seemed as if it must be

impossible – for to kill her father must be the work of an
enemy, so how could *I* have done it? It was to be unkind and
untrue to her – so how could *my* hands have been able to
do such a thing? I could not understand it. For Miss Gwenllian
I would have gladly sacrificed everything I possessed – happiness, health, life itself – then how could I have been so
untrue to myself as to bring this great sorrow upon her?
Could it indeed be *I* who had taken the life of one she loved
and depended on? Alas! If so, I had taken from her what I
could never restore to her nor make up for to her – never,
never!

Then my bewildered thoughts became collected enough
for me to attend to what the people around me were saying
as they talked over what had just been read to them.

Their voices sounded to me strange and far off, and
somehow different from what they had been before; but yet
I understood all they said.

'Well, well!' said one, 'I wonder shall they catch the man
as shot him?'

'Catch him?' exclaimed Griffiths, who had laid down the
paper to discuss the matter at his ease; 'catch him, do you
say? You shall take your oath as they shall do that – most
like as they have done it already! You was not suppose as a
magistrate shall be shot and the man as did it go free? I was
not wonder if they shall hang all the lot of prisoners, so as
to make sure not to miss the right one!'

'Look you farther on in the paper, Griffy,' said the landlord;
'maybe there shall be some more about it somewhere else.'

On this Griffiths again took up *The Budget* and began
studying it, and presently exclaimed: 'Yes – here's more of
it now. Didn't I tell you as they was sure to have the man?
Here it be! They do know exactly who it was as shot the
Squire, and where he do live, and all about him; so no doubt
but what they do have him safe in gaol by now. Listen you

here.' And then he read the following out of *The Bridgend Budget*:

'It has been discovered that the murderer of Mr Tudor is a young man named Evan Williams, whose home is at Upper Killay. A discharged gun, having the words, E. Williams, Upper Killay, carved on the stock, was picked up close to where the fight took place, and as no second gunshot was heard during the combat, there seems to be no doubt that it was by means of this weapon that Mr Tudor met his fate. The police, on proceeding to the home of the said Evan Williams, found he had already disappeared; but we feel sure that he will not long elude the vigilance of that acute and intelligent body, the county police. Some three years ago, before the Tudor family went abroad, the murderer appears to have been treated with great kindness by Miss Tudor and other members of the family, of which kindness he was most absolutely unworthy. For the murder seems to have been a wilful one, and not a mere chance shot into the *mêlée*. Two of the police, who were on the spot, affirm that they saw the murderer stand still and take a deliberate aim at his victim – there being at the time so bright a light from the blazing turnpike-gate and house as to make it impossible for Williams not to have recognised the gentleman at whom he fired. It appears, therefore, that for some unknown reason Williams purposely selected as his victim one who had been in former day his benefactor, instead of venting his bloodthirsty fury on any of the other opponents who were engaged against him. It is supposed that he must have had some grudge against Mr Tudor, and took this opportunity of gratifying his long-cherished desire for vengeance. We can only say that the vindictiveness and ingratitude displayed in this atrocious murder are truly terrible, and—'

I could stand this no longer, but got up and staggered out of the house; leaving Tom to pay our bill and make some

excuse about my being suddenly taken ill. Fortunately the
other men were too much engrossed with Griffiths and the
news to pay any attention to our proceedings.

I walked for about a mile out of the town without saying
a word, while Tom followed me, very much puzzled as to
what had come over me. Then I turned round to him with
my mind fully made up.

'Good-bye, Tom,' I said; 'get you away into the mountains,
as we did settle to do. I do not be coming with you.'

'Not coming!' cried Tom, in utmost astonishment. 'Why
what have come to you, man? And what shall you be going
to do with yourself then?'

'I do be going back to Swansea,' replied I.

'Back to Swansea!' echoed he; 'man alive, be you gone
mad? For certain sure they shall get hold of you there and
hang you!'

'Can't help it if they do,' returned I; 'all I do know is, that
I must get to Penfawr and see Miss Gwenllian, and tell her
as I was not know it was him when I was shoot him – and
as it was not true what that there lying newspaper do say.'

Tom stared to hear me speak like this, and thought I was
out of my senses. He laughed at me, scolded me, reasoned
with me, did everything he could to make me change my
mind, but it was not the least use.

No power on earth could turn me from what I had settled
to do, for it seemed to me the only way by which I could
possibly hope to put myself right in Miss Gwenllian's eyes,
and make her believe that, even if I had killed her father, yet
it had been wholly an accident.

If she saw me myself come back to explain it to her, then
she would surely believe that I spoke the truth, and believe
in my sorrow for having injured her, and forgive me.

When Tom found that I was immovable he wanted to come
with me, saying that I was not fit to go alone, and that he

should come and see what became of me and take his chance
of being caught. But I told him how foolish that would be,
and talked about Martha, and told him it was his business
to escape and try and make a home for her; and so at last I
persuaded him to set off alone towards the mountains and
to leave me to go back alone.

You see his circumstances and mine were very different.
He was bound to take care of himself for the sake of a woman
who loved him and whom he loved; but I had no woman
to love me; and all that I had before me was to go and see
the one whom I cared for more than all others, and to ask
her – not that she should care for me, but merely that she
should not hate me, or, if she could not help doing so, yet
at least that she should not wrong me with a deeper hatred
than I deserved. Till this was accomplished I must not let
myself be arrested; and afterwards – my head was too dizzy
to make plans for afterwards; it did not seem to me that it
mattered much what became of me one way or other.

If they caught me I supposed they would hang me – but
really that was a matter as to which I could not be bothering
myself then.

CHAPTER XVI

Before noon on the next day I was again near Swansea, after having walked the whole distance from Bridgend without making any stop except for a few hours when I slept under a hayrick. Stupid and bewildered as my mind was, I had yet sense enough to understand that if I were to be made prisoner before I could speak to Miss Gwenllian, then the whole object of my journey would be frustrated; therefore I did not pass through the town of Swansea, but skirted round it, avoiding houses and people and high-roads as much as possible. At last I stood at the edge of the Penfawr grounds, having as I believed got thus far without having been recognised by anyone. I climbed over the fence that enclosed the Tudor property, and began to make my way across fields and copses in the direction of the house.

Since the day before when I had heard that horrible newspaper read out at Bridgend I had been almost like a man walking in his sleep, for I was wholly engrossed by the longing that had come over me to see Miss Gwenllian, to tell her that I had not recognised her father when I shot him, and to beg her to forgive me; this one idea had excluded all others from my mind, and it have never occurred to me that I had anything to do but to walk straight to Penfawr and say what I had to say. But now that I was so near the end of my journey it suddenly struck me that if Miss Gwenllian knew who I was she would perhaps refuse to see me, and that I must try for her not to find out my name till I should have accomplished my object and justified myself. But how could I manage this if she recognised me directly she saw me? I was pondering

over this knotty point when I jumped over a hedge and found
myself face to face with one of the Penfawr gamekeepers.
He was a complete stranger to me, but, being naturally surprised to meet a disreputable-looking, travel-stained man such
as I was in the midst of the grounds, he roughly asked me
what business brought me there.

I was quite disconcerted at this sudden meeting and
questioning, and hesitated before answering. 'I do be after
no harm,' said I at last; 'I do be only just going to the big house
to say something to the young lady about some business.'

No doubt my appearance and my hesitation in speaking
were both a good deal against me; and the keeper evidently
looked upon me with the utmost suspicion.

'A likely story for me to believe!' he replied. 'People as
wants to go to the house to see the young lady goes there
by the proper roads instead of coming across country and
breaking down the fences like this! 'Tis a deal more like that
the rabbits and the rabbit-holes be the business as brings you
here. Stop you a moment for me to see how many rabbit-
wires you have about you.'

Saying this he caught hold of me and began turning my
pockets inside out and searching me for anything that could
convict me of being a poacher. To this I submitted quite
patiently, making sure that as soon as he had satisfied himself
of the groundlessness of his suspicions he would allow me
to go to the house without further hindrance. But to my great
disappointment I found that he still opposed my going on,
even after he had completed his fruitless search.

'I don't believe as you've any business here anyways,' said
he; 'so come you along with me till I see you off the premises.
I don't mean to have all the idle tramps in the country think
that they are to come sauntering about these here grounds
just when and how they like now that the old Squire is dead!
Come along now, and don't let me catch you trespassing here
again.'

'Oh, but indeed and I must see the young lady,' replied I eagerly; ''tis so true as true what I was tell you! I do come to speak to her about something that do matter very much for her to know. Only I was have the bad luck to lose my way, and 'tis for that as you do find me here in the middle of the fields.'

The keeper paused and scratched his head meditatively. He did not altogether believe me, and did not at all approve of my looks; but as there was nothing very unlikely about my story, he had no sufficient excuse to turn me neck and crop off the premises, as he would have liked to do; therefore, after a few minutes' consideration, he grunted out sulkily:

'Well! If so be you *must* go to the house, why I suppose as you must. But I'll come along there with you, and make sure that you really do have business to take you there. And if I catch you in having been telling me lies – why 'twill be the worse for you, my man.'

And then he accompanied me to Penfawr House, keeping close beside me all the way, and watching me most carefully for fear I should try and run away. When we reached the house, he sent in word to Miss Gwenllian that someone wanted to see her about something particular; and then I was taken to wait in the servants'-hall until she should come to see me.

And so this was the end of it all! Here was I, who had looked forward to Miss Gwenllian's return as the greatest possible happiness; who had worshipped the thought of her ever since I had known her; who had been ready to take whatever she wished as a law to be obeyed by me; here was I, I say, waiting to meet her again after so long a time, with my mind wholly given up to the one longing that I might get her to forgive me for having killed her father! How could such a thing have come to pass? What had happened seemed so horrible, and so utterly unlike anything that I had ever imagined or dreamt of as being possible, that I could hardly believe it to be true.

But the strangeness of all this did not strike me so much just then. Everything was swallowed up and lost in my anxiety to accomplish my purpose, and to say what I had to say to her. I had hardly given a thought to anything else since I had left Bridgend, and had almost worked myself into a fever with my impatience to get it done. Yet now that the moment when I should speak to her was so near, I began to dread it terribly; I could not imagine what words I should use; I had hardly courage enough to meet her.

I did not have very long to wait before the door opened and she came into the room.

I saw she did not know me again; and though I had been scheming a short time before how I should manage to tell her what I wanted before she should find out who I was, yet when the moment came that I was in her presence and found she did not recognise me, it seemed to freeze the words back from my lips, and made me more nervous and frightened than ever. Of course I had altered a good deal since last she had seen me, and it was not to be supposed that she had thought of me and kept my face continually before her memory, as I had done in respect of her. But I forgot this difference between us, and her not at once remembering me gave me a strange feeling of sinking and disappointment. Her beautiful brown eyes looked just the same as in the old times, when I had first seen them in the carriage with the runaway horses, coming along the road at Upper Killay; and I should have known her again anywhere, though she had grown taller and handsomer and statelier than she used to be. She looked very pale and sad in the deep mourning which she wore, and the first glance showed me that she had been crying; but I think she did not wish that to be seen, for she kept her eyes fixed on the ground after looking at me once as she came into the room.

'You want to see me about something, don't you?' asked she, speaking in the old kind voice that sounded to me like beautiful music heard long ago.

'Yes, miss,' answered I, shuffling about and stammering; 'if you please, miss—'

Here I stopped short. In my nervousness and excitement I had quite forgotten the words I had meant to use, and I kept vainly trying to remember them, whilst she stood before me waiting patiently for me to go on.

The disappointment of her not recognising me, seemed to have made me no better than a fool, and when at last I spoke, the only thing I could say was: 'Was you not know who I do be then, miss?'

She raised her eyes from the ground, looked at me for an instant, and then answered:

'No, I don't. But I seem to remember your voice too, and I daresay I shall recollect all about you directly. Tell me your name, and where you come from.'

My wits were clean gone; and in my stupidity I could think of nothing better than just to answer whatever she asked me, so I stammered out:

'I be Evan Williams, from Upper Killay miss; I be come—'

She started at this, and drew a little farther away from me, exclaiming: 'My father's murderer! Stop – hush! Why have you forced yourself upon me like this? Surely you can understand that I have no wish to see you. As you have come here of your own accord, I would rather not give you up to the police; but after what you have done, you cannot expect me ever again to have anything to do with you.'

So saying she turned away and opened the door to go out. But how could I let her go like that before I had yet told her what I had come so far to say? I sprang forward and took hold of her dress, crying out to her that she must stay and hear me. But she only thought that I meant to do her some harm with my violence, and called out for help, which at once brought the gamekeeper and footman to the spot.

My despair gave me back the words that I had not said before.

'Indeed to goodness, and I never guessed it to be he when I fired!' cried I. But my words had come to me too late; for the two men were exclaiming and making so much noise as they seized hold of me and dragged me away from Miss Gwenllian, and made me let go of her gown, that she did not hear rightly what I said, and fancied I had meant to threaten her. All she said was: 'So you would have treated me as you did my poor father? Oh, Evan! I would never have believed it of you.'

At this moment Miss Elizabeth Tudor appeared upon the scene. She came hurrying into the servants'-hall exclaiming:

'Gwenllian, Gwenllian dear! Where are you? Don't be frightened my love – but I came to tell you that that villain Evan Williams has been seen—' Here she stopped abruptly as she saw me in the hands of the two servants.

'Why, gracious goodness me, that is never him, is it?' cried she. And then she went on when Miss Gwenllian had given a sign of assent: 'Oh, whatever has he been doing here? Hadn't you better come away, dear, for fear the wretch might break loose and murder us all? What a horrible creature he must be – and what an escape we've had! No doubt Providence settles everything for the best. But for all that, perhaps we had better go away for fear something might happen.' Then she addressed the footman, saying: 'Hold him tight, Charles, and the police will be here to help you in a minute – they're close by, I know.' And then she went on again to Miss Gwenllian!

'Don't be frightened, my love; there is no reason to be alarmed any longer, I do hope and trust. Someone who knew this wretched man by sight saw him enter our grounds a short time ago, and at once went off to warn the police of it, and then came to tell us, and that's how I heard of it. The police are searching for him in all directions, and will be sure to be here immediately. I'm sure it was most kind and thoughtful of the man who told the police that the villain had been seen, and I shall take care that he is the better for his kindness.'

(I suppose that the old lady was too flurried to remember that there was a reward offered for my apprehension, which was large enough to make it quite worth while for a poor man to try and earn it – so that probably kindness to her had very little to do in the matter.)

She went hurrying on her words one after the other, and hardly stopping to take breath: 'Of course we can't know for certain as yet what brought the scoundrel here – but I feel very little doubt that he meant to set the house on fire and murder every one of us. Mercifully his atrocious design is frustrated – you see Providence settles everything for the best! Don't you recollect how I always warned you against him, Gwenllian, from the first time that ever you had to do with him? *I* saw what wickedness was in him from the very first – what good could be expected from a boy who refused to say the Catechism, and who had never been baptized, not been to church, nor— nor—? I do declare there's a policeman passing the window at this very moment. As I always have said, and always shall say, no doubt Providence settles everything for the best!'

With this she flung open the window to beckon in the policeman; and then hurried off, cackling away like an old hen as she went, and carrying off her niece with her, while I was left in the hands of the servants and police.

As for me, I made no resistance at all, neither when first the servants had laid hold of me, nor yet when the constable snapped a pair of handcuffs together upon my wrists. I was quite stupefied by all that had happened, and hardly noticed what was being done to me. I was like a man in a dream – a bad dream from which he cannot rouse himself, while yet he has a half knowledge of what is going on around him.

So I had thrown away my chance of escape for nothing! I had come back from Bridgend into the midst of my enemies, simply and solely in order to tell Miss Gwenllian the truth about her father's death, and thus stand right in her eyes – as I hoped – and this was what had come of it all! She had not heard what I had meant to tell her – she had imagined that my object in seeing her had been to harm or kill her. She had gone away in this belief – I should never see her again. I myself was a prisoner, and was certain to be hanged! It was hard upon me – bitterly hard.

If she could have heard me speak and have forgiven me, I should not have minded so much: but as it was – why I must die, and she would never know the truth.

It was no fault of hers – I had only my own stupidity and nervousness to blame for my failure. What a fool I have been! But there was no help for it now; and then Miss Elizabeth Tudor's last words began to run in my head strangely: 'No doubt Providence settles everything for the best.' I kept saying this over and over again to myself, in a dull sort of way; and presently I took to speculating about it, and wondering if it could be true.

Did Providence really settle everything? Certainly it was not I, nor yet any friend of mine, who settled things; for no single thing that had happened that I had wished or intended. Perhaps that was because Providence settled them – as Miss Elizabeth said – and if so, it was very evident that Providence was no friend to me. Providence! What did the word mean? And why should Providence have such a spite against me? Well! The only comfort was that when Providence had done its worst to me and I should be dead, then there would be an end of it all. It was quite clear that what Providence had settled for me was, that I was to be misjudged and hated by

Miss Gwenllian, and that I was to be hung; as Providence seemed to be stronger than me, there was no use my grumbling, and I had better think of something else.

But to think of anything else just then was quite out of my power; and I kept repeating the words again and again in a mazed way, and trying dully to understand them: No doubt Providence settles everything for the best. How could it be for the best that I should have shot Squire Tudor, and that Miss Gwenllian should hate me, and that I should be hanged? For whom was it the best? Certainly not for me, nor yet for the old Squire and his daughter. Was it for Providence, then, that it was for the best? Ah, perhaps that was it – for of course everyone knew that Providence settles everything for the best!

So the words kept ringing in my head, and would not leave me. Our steps kept time to them, as they marched me along the road from Penfawr to Swansea gaol. A syllable went to each step; and though I tried to change the beat once or twice, by shuffling my feet and stepping out of time, it was no use – the words were too strong for me, and forced my steps to keep time to them whether I liked it or not.

When I got to the prison and was shut up in a cell, I thought that perhaps I might get rid of the odious words, now that I was sitting quiet. But no! Outside in the passage there was a great clock, and its heavy regular ticking kept on repeating steadily and incessantly: 'No doubt Providence settles everything for the best.'

The detestable words had taken possession of me. I could not forget them, I could not get away from them, I could think of nothing except them and the clock, whose monotonous ticking hammered them perseveringly into my brain. I forgot Upper Killay – Rebecca – Bill Jones – Miss Gwenllian – Tom Davies – I forgot everything except this one sentence of Miss Elizabeth's. Night came, and I longed to go to sleep, for

I was utterly weary both in body and mind; but I found I had not a chance of sleeping as long as the clock went on ticking those haunting words. I was burning and aching all over, and as I tossed and tumbled about on my bed, it suddenly occurred to me that perhaps if I were to say the words out loud myself, that might silence the clock. So I tried doing this, and then I found to my horror that when I had begun saying them aloud I could not leave off, but must go on saying them in exact time with the horrible ticking that was keeping me awake. I no longer thought of any meaning in the words, but went on repeating them mechanically, though I was unspeakably weary of them and loathed them intensely, and had just sense enough left to desire from the bottom of my soul that I could finish my task and go to sleep.

But my longing for rest was in vain. I could not stop, and I knew it. So long as that clock continued to tick, so long must my tongue go on saying the same words that the ticking said. And then I felt as if I must choke if I stayed lying down any longer while there was so much talking to be done, so I was obliged to sit bolt upright on my bed.

Thus I spent the whole night sitting up on the bed with my eyes wide open and staring towards the clock, and repeating incessantly: 'No – doubt – Providence – settles – every – thing – for – the – best;' without ever stopping, even for one single instant.

At last the dreary hours of darkness were over, and the morning light came. But the light did not enable me to cease from my task – my fate was settled, and I knew quite well what it was: that I should never be able to stop saying the words until someone should shoot the clock and forgive me. Ah, why would not someone take pity on me and come and do this? It seemed such a small thing to ask, and yet it would bring me such happiness, for then I could die and be quiet at last. I was so very very tired of my work, and yet I must continue it without a moment's pause unless some kind person would come and release me.

What if no one should ever come to my assistance? That would be too terrible. For in that case I should have to go on for ever, and I should never be let to die and be at rest in the grave like everyone else is. As the worst of it was, that presently the horrible ticking began to go faster. As it quickened its pace so did the words go faster also; and then I was compelled to say the words faster likewise, so that I might keep up with the clock. It was terribly hard work to do this, and I felt almost maddened by it.

And then the sun began to stream into the cell, and I found out what made the clock go at such a rate. For then I was able to see quite clearly through the walls to the clock outside – on which were perched two magpies that hopped up and down and chattered in perfect time with the ticking, and I not only saw the clock but also right into its works. One of the wheels was Smith, with a white face and the blood trickling down one side, as I had seen him lying on Fairwood Moor, and he was running round and round as fast as he could go to keep away from another wheel, which was Rees Hughes, and rushed round after Smith, trying to get in reach to hit him each time that the wheels had finished one whole turn. The faster the Smith wheel ran away the faster the Hughes wheel ran after it, and of course that made it plain enough why the clock was going so fast. The two wheels looked so droll that I daresay I should have laughed at them, only that I had no breath to spare with repeating the words at such a tremendous rate.

And all the time that Smith and Hughes chased round and round after each other, they were calling out something. And the chattering of the magpies also sounded like words. And when I by-and-by discovered what the words were, I found that what the two men were shouting, and the two magpies chattering, was the very same sentence that the clock ticked and that I had to say: 'No doubt Providence settles everything for the best!'

So we all went on together – ticking, chattering, and calling out these words together without stopping for a second; and getting constantly faster because the two men would go so fast – which imposed upon the magpies, the clock, and me, the necessity of hurrying terribly to keep up with them.

CHAPTER XVII

It was many weeks after this before I was conscious of anything again, and then I found myself lying on one of the beds in the prison hospital, too weak to move from one side to the other without help.

I had been dangerously ill with brain-fever. When the gaoler went to my cell on the next day after I had been put in prison, he had found me sitting bolt upright in the bed, staring hard at the wall of the cell and stretching out my arms towards it, and shouting out some words or other so loud and fast that he could not make out what they were. Finding that I did not know him or pay the least attention to him, he had fetched the doctor, who had had me moved into the hospital, and there I had tossed about ever since in a high fever.

At first I felt too ill and tired to trouble my head much as to any past or future events; but as the days passed on and I began to regain a little strength, I began also to remember what had happened before my illness. I wondered, in a feeble sort of fashion, whether any of my family or Bill Jones knew where I was, and, if so, why they did not come and see me. But when I said something about it to the doctor one day, he said that I was not strong enough to be allowed to see any visitors yet. So I waited on very contentedly. I was still too weak to get excited or impatient about anything; and every feeling of hope for the future or possible pleasure in life was utterly beaten out of me by my sickness, and by my recollection that I had failed to justify myself to Miss Gwenllian, and that she regarded me as the wilful murderer of her father.

Then, too, I remembered that I must surely be condemned to the gallows, and I thought it was more cruelty than kindness to take care of me and send the doctor to make me well in order that I might be hung in the end! I would rather if they had let me die in the fever.

But though these things worried me in a hazy and far-off sort of way, yet I was too much pulled down and exhausted to take them very much to heart, and was quite satisfied to let the days drift on, and never to look beyond the present moment.

Presently, however, I got strong enough to see father and mother and Martha, when they came to see me; but Bill Jones did not come too; and when I asked where he was, and why he did not pay me a visit, they did not seem to want to talk about him, merely saying that he was quite well, and then hurrying on to speak about something else, which rather surprised me. At last, however, the day came when I was so far recovered as to be considered well enough to hear what had become of him. Very astonishing the story was, too, for it appeared that our Bill Jones, whom I had picked up in Swansea Market, was none other than Squire Tudor's son Owen, who was believed to have been drowned in his infancy. So that Bill Jones was Miss Gwenllian's brother, and the lawful heir to the Penfawr property; which, being entailed in the male line, would otherwise have gone to a distant cousin of the late Squire's.

But I must begin at the beginning of the story.

At the time when Owen Tudor was born, there was a woman named Jones living in Swansea, who was a regular thief and beggar by profession, and who had made friends with Mrs Tudor's nurse, and had persuaded her, at various times, to steal one or two small articles belonging to her mistress, by which means the nurse was to some degree in Jones's power.

The baby Owen was always beautifully dressed, with a

good deal of satin and lace about his clothes, and always had tied round his neck a solid gold heart-shaped locket with a curious device upon it in emeralds. This locket was a Tudor heirloom, and had been supposed, in old times, to be some kind of charm that brought luck to its owner, and it was Mrs Tudor's wish that her baby-boy should never be without it.

Well, Jones being short of money, and casting covetous eyes on his smart attire and locket, proposed to the nurse that they should steal the child and its clothes; the clothes and locket they would sell, she said, that the child himself she would take for her own – it would be a help to her in begging as long as it was little, and when it grew up she would make him useful to her in other ways. At first the nurse was shocked at the idea, and would on no account consent to such a thing; but at last she gave way, on Jones threatening that otherwise she would let Mrs Tudor know of the thefts that the nurse had already committed.

Accordingly, one morning, the child was duly handed over to Jones, while the nurse wetted herself from head to foot in a stream of water, and went back to Penfawr with her story of the child having been swept away by the sea.

One thing which Jones insisted on having done was that the nurse, who was a well-educated woman, should write on a piece of paper an account of the transaction, and state who the child really was, and this document Jones kept in her own possession. Why she should have insisted on this seems very strange, unless she may have had some idea of making money, by restoring the boy to his parents at some time or other. She sold the child's clothes and handed over a share of the profits to the nurse, as agreed upon; but the locket she failed to sell, because the man who usually took such things off her hands would not give as large a price for it as she thought she ought to have, and she did not venture to take it to any respectable jeweller, for fear of his wanting to know how it came into her possession; therefore she kept it by her for the present.

After this affair the nurse remained in service for a few years longer, and then married the farmer named Smith, of whose murder on Fairwood Common I told you at the commencement of my story.

The stolen boy lived on with Mrs Jones, who called him Bill and gave out that he was her son; but by-and-by she seems for some reason or other to have taken a great dislike to him, and sent him to sea in the *Nancy Jones* instead of keeping him at home with her as she meant to have done. When her friend Mrs Smith asked her why she had done this, she only answered:

'I do have took against that brat till I can't abear the very sight of him, and I do want him to be out of my way for a bit. Maybe though as I shall get fond of him when he do grow up and bring me in a bit of money, for I do mostly like them as be useful to me – yes, indeed!'

For some time after this Mrs Smith saw and heard nothing more of Jones, until one day a Gower carrier, who had been into Swansea, brought Mrs Smith a message to say that Jones was very ill, and begged Mrs Smith to go and see her at once. The next day Mrs Smith could not well manage to go to Swansea herself, so she told her husband, who was going to sell a horse at the market, to go for her, and find out what Jones wanted of her. He went to Jones's residence, a wretched, tumble-down little house, in one of the worst alleys of Swansea, but by the time he got there Jones was almost dead. Before her death, however, she managed to give him a small box, telling him it was of the greatest importance, and that he must give it to his wife, who would know all about it, and of what great value the contents were.

It seems strange that Jones should have taken such trouble about preserving the proofs of the boy's identity; but possibly her conscience may have troubled her on her deathbed, and she may have had an idea that by this means she was making some kind of amends for her crime. However, that is mere conjecture, and of course no one can be sure what her reasons really were.

But, notwithstanding her carefulness, the little box never reached the person for whom it was intended, for it was on the evening of that very same day that Smith was attacked, and robbed, and mortally wounded on Fairwood by Rees Hughes and Tom Davies. Rees Hughes, who had heard Smith boasting at the public-house about some treasure that he was carrying, came upon the box which Mrs Jones had trusted to him, and guessed it to be the important parcel that Smith had talked so big about. Thinking that its contents must be very valuable, he secreted it from his partner, Tom Davies, so that he might not have to go shares in it. When he came to open it he was much disappointed to find nothing but two papers with writing on them, and a heart-shaped bit of metal which was too dirty for him to tell what it was. Being unable to read, he did not know what the writings were about, and had at first a great mind to burn them. Finally, however, he determined to keep them on chance of their being useful to him some day, for, thought he, if they were *not* important to someone, why should they have been done up so carefully in the box? And why should anyone have made a fuss about them? And if they *were* important, he might as well keep them in his possession, and try and turn them to account in course of time. The box and its contents being small and light, he always carried it with him for safety, and thus he had it upon him at the time when he was wounded and captured at the fight at Pontardulais; but as he did not know what the writings might be about, and did not care to have the box found on him, for fear of its getting him into a worse scrape than he was in already, he managed to hide it away in a corner of the

shed in which he and the other prisoners were kept on that
night until the arrival of the soldiers.

The wound he had received was a very serious one, and
fatal inflammation set in. The poor fellow was quite miserable
at having to die in the midst of strangers and enemies, without
one friendly face to comfort him, and begged so hard for Bill
Jones to be let to come and see him that his request was
granted, and Bill was with him as much as possible up to
the time of his death. Rough, selfish, surly, unloving, as Rees
Hughes had always been, he had always been strangely fond
of Bill, and to Bill he imparted the secret of the box, of how
he had come by it, and of where he had hidden it, and told
Bill that he was to have it for his own, and make anything
that he could out of it.

As soon as Bill had time, after Hughes's death, he went
over to Pontardulais and found the box; and then, not being
able to read himself, and feeling curious about the matter,
he one day took the two papers to the minister of Three
Crosses, and got him to read them to him.

One of the papers contained the account of Owen Tudor's
abduction, and the other only had these words written on
it: 'The boy is now at sea in the *Pride of Towy*'; which was
dated at the time of Mrs Jones's death, she having got a
neighbour to write this down for her, and enclosed it in the
box when she felt herself to be dying.

Directly Bill heard these papers read, and the names of the
vessels, he pricked up his ears, for he remembered having
sailed in the *Nancy Jones*, and having been at sea in the *Pride
of Towy* at the time when his supposed mother died. The
minister, seeing the importance of all this to the Tudor family,
took the box and its contents to Penfawr; and there Miss
Elizabeth at once recognised the locket, as being the one that
Owen Tudor had had round his neck on the day that he had
been lost.

The matter was then put into the hands of the family lawyer, who went down to Gower to see the widow Smith. She would at first say nothing, except that the baby had been swept away by the sea; but when she found how much was already known, and when she saw the account of the child's abduction in her own handwriting, she confessed everything. And thus, as the story came out, bit by bit, it was proved that Owen Tudor and Bill Jones were one and the same person. For his own recollections were confirmed by people at Neath and at Swansea, who knew him to be the same boy who had always been considered as Mrs Jones's son, and who had been away at sea in the *Pride of Towy* when she died.

All this was quite enough to take away my breath, and it was some time before I could altogether take it in. To think that our Bill Jones should turn out to be a rich man, and a gentleman born, and Miss Gwenllian's brother after all! And what queer things seemed to have resulted from that fight at Pontardulais! It had taken one master from Penfawr, and given it another; taught Bill to know who his father was, and at the same time taken that father from him; deprived Miss Gwenllian of her father, and been the means of restoring to her her brother; had avenged the murder of Smith by killing Rees Hughes, and at the same time had made known the crime of Smith's wife.

One comfort to me out of all this was that, as Owen Tudor had known how entirely ignorant I was of who it was that I had killed at the Pontardulais 'pike, he would be sure to make this known to his sister; so that she would no longer consider me as the wilful murderer of her father, and would perhaps forgive me at last. And not only did he do this and bring Miss Gwenllian to see me in prison, but also, he and she got a clever lawyer to defend me when my trial came on, and did all they could to help me in every way; and so between them all they managed to get me off from being hung, and I was transported for life to this place instead.

Fifteen years ago it was that I was sent here – fifteen long and dreary years, during which I have been cut off from that liberty to which every man is born, and which gives a sweetness that nothing else can give to life; and have been cut off also from all the people and places that I loved. But after all I ought not to complain; for if I had not insisted on going back to see Miss Gwenllian from Bridgend, I should doubtless have made my escape, and a man has no right to grumble at what has been entirely his own fault.

In those fifteen years I have had time enough to look back at my past life, and to reason about it almost as though it were the life of someone else, and not my own. It seems to me that my prison life has at any rate taught me patience – for a man is always patient when he cannot avoid his trouble, but has to bear it whether he likes or not – and so I am patient enough now. I sometimes think that if I could have learnt the lesson sooner, and been more willing to put up with what I disliked, then perhaps I might have escaped this weary confinement altogether. Patience is what we all have to learn sooner or later; and if, as Miss Elizabeth said, Providence settles everything for the best, it may be that my hateful prison life had been for the best for me in reality, because it has taught me that necessary virtue.

And yet even if so, it seems almost like a waste of pain that only one person should be the better for such bitter sorrow and disappointment and unhappiness as I have undergone; and that no one except myself is to profit by all my tedious suffering. However, I have had no choice in the matter – it is not I who am responsible for it.

Possibly you may say that I was altogether wrong in the old days, and that I brought my misfortunes on myself. But was the fault wholly mine? Might I not have been taught to know better?

If the rich would try to civilise the poor – not merely by

giving them money, and blankets, and coals at random, but by going amongst them with a real and unaffected sympathy that forgets differences of rank, and sees in each poor person a fellow-creature with the same faults, virtues, needs, and feelings as a gentleman has – then poor men would not be imbued with that feeling of natural enmity and distrust towards their superiors which had a very great deal to do with the Rebecca riots.

Granted that Rees Hughes and Phil Jenkins, and the rest of us at Killay were rough, wild drunkards, thieves, and worse, what chance had we had of being anything different? No doubt Miss Gwenllian did do something for me; but one person cannot make up for the evils of a whole system, and it is the system that is to blame – the system of narrowness and of pride, and of exclusiveness, and of no one doing anything for another, unless there is something to be gained in return. This it is that makes rich and poor natural born enemies to each other; and it is the rich who should make the first attempts to break down these barriers, because they have the responsibility of that superior knowledge and education which come to them as a birthright.

But all these things concern me now no more; for you tell me, doctor, that I shall not live much longer, and my own feelings seem to say the same.

I should like to have seen Miss Gwenllian once more before I die – but that cannot be; so I want you, as the next best thing, to find her out when you go back to England, and to tell her my story as I have told it to you. I should like for her to know what my life really was, because it was she who made so much difference in it. Tell her, that although it is so many years since I have seen her, yet that the recollection of her is as fresh in my memory as though I had parted from her only this moment.

I am grateful to her, not only for her goodness to me, but

also for what she did for my family. For after I was transported she and her brother looked after them, and arranged things and paid their expenses for them when they went out to America to take Martha there to marry Tom Davies. He got safely to Liverpool at last, and embarked from there for America – as no doubt I should have done too, if I had not heard that newspaper read out at Bridgend – and from America he sent back to Martha to come and marry him. I believe they are all thriving there capitally now – at least to judge by their letters, which are always contented, and speaking of prosperity.

As for the traitor, Pugh Morgan, I have heard what became of him through letters and newspapers which have reached me at various times from some of my old friends.

You may remember how Martha was struck with the idea that Pugh might have betrayed us through jealousy of Tom, and how I sent her to communicate her suspicions to Jenkin Thomas – I being at that moment starting on my flight, and having no time to see him myself. When she had told Jenkin he spoke about it to one or two other Rebeccas, and then they began to make secret inquiries, which revealed that Pugh had certainly been in Swansea on the day of the fight at Pontardulais 'pike; and furthermore, that on the same day, a man answering to his description, specially noticeable by reason of his squeaky voice, had been closeted with the head of the police, and had not left his house till next day.

This was fatal to Morgan.

Very good care had been taken that he should know nothing of the suspicions and inquiries respecting him; but his sense of guilt seems to have made him uneasy, for he said that he was going to leave the neighbourhood altogether, and go and settle somewhere in England, and he made all preparations for selling his house and furniture. The only thing that delayed him was his inability to tear himself away from Martha, and he again and again put off his departure that he might make one more attempt to get her to change her mind and marry him.

At last one day he was suddenly missing, and no one saw him again, or heard anything from him. People supposed that he had at last carried out his long-talked-of plan, and taken himself off for good and all. Yet they said it was rather odd, too, that he had left everything in his house exactly as if he were coming back to it, and that he never sent to fetch his goods away. But then he always was fond of mysterious goings and comings; and people soon left off talking about his sudden disappearance, and thought no more about him till a few months afterwards, when something happened which recalled him to their minds.

I have already mentioned Clyne Wood, which is close to Killay and runs down to the sea. Well, this wood is full of deep pits, where workings for coal have been begun and then deserted because of the coal failing; and as these old pits are generally overgrown with brambles and long grass and bushes at the mouth, it is a hard matter to see them; and being usually more or less full of water, they are very nasty places for any living creature to get into, and many a dog has been lost in them when taken there by gentlemen out shooting. It happened that a gentleman was one day leaning over one of these deserted coal-pits, and trying to look into it, when the gun he was holding slipped out of his hand and fell in; and as he set great store by this gun, he took a good deal of trouble to get it back again. To accomplish this he had to get ropes and ladders, and send someone down into the pit; and at the bottom was found the remains of a man's body. A thick cord fastened the hands and feet together, and proved that he must have been thrown in by someone else, and had not fallen in by accident. The face was quite unrecognisable, as the flesh had been almost all eaten away from the bones by rats; but on dragging the mud and slime at the bottom of the pit, a tin box was discovered bearing Pugh Morgan's name upon it, and also a knife that was known to have belonged to him, and it was generally believed that the body must have been his.

How he came there was never known, but I think I can make a pretty good guess at it. The men who had been betrayed by Pugh Morgan at Pontardulais, and who had sworn to be revenged on the traitor if ever they should discover him, were men with fierce passions who would not fail to keep their oath of vengeance. I can imagine that a party of these men may have got hold of Pugh in some out-of-the-way place, or possibly may have seized him at night in his own cottage, have stifled his cries for help, tied him hand and foot, carried him gagged and helpless to Clyne Wood, flung him down the coal-pit, and there left him to drown if it should be full of water, or, if it should be dry, to linger on half smashed by the fall till he died of hunger, as a fitting reward for his treachery. Whether it were really so or not I cannot tell; but at all events nothing more was ever seen or heard of Pugh Morgan – and no man may expect to live securely and die in peace who has betrayed to prison and death those who trusted in him.

And now the story of the life of my old self is ended, and I trust you to tell it to Miss Gwenllian for me if ever you have the opportunity. And if ever you should find yourself at Swansea, and if you go to the top of one of the hills to the west of the town, and see the view from there – looking across the bright blue sea to Devonshire in one direction, and seeing, as you turn round, Lundy Island, and Cefn Bryn, and the distant mountains in Pembrokeshire, Carmarthenshire, Breconshire, and the Swansea valley, and the coast beyond Neath, and across to the Dunraven cliffs – then perhaps you will be able to understand why I have so pined and longed for my own home and country ever since I have been here, and why it grieves me that I cannot see it again just once more before I die; for I have never seen any other place that has seemed to me so beautiful.

EDITOR'S EPILOGUE

I was physician to one of our convict establishments when I made acquaintance with the hero of this story; he was attacked by an incurable disease, and died not long after he had finished dictating to me the foregoing pages.

MORGANWG.

The Honno Classics series is an imprint which brings books by women writers from Wales in English, long since out of print, to a new generation of readers. The following are also available in the Honno Classics series:

Queen of the Rushes
by Allen Raine

With an Introduction by Katie Gramich

Allen Raine (Anne Adaliza Puddicombe) was one of the most popular authors of the turn of the century, with her books selling over a million copies in Britain alone. *Queen of the Rushes*, first published in 1906, has been out of print for over fifty years, but now Allen Raine's powerful and accomplished novel can be enjoyed again. Set in a seaside village in West Wales at the time of the 1904 Revival, the novel relates the enthralling tale of the lives and complex loves of Gildas, Nancy, Gwenifer and Captain Jack. Eminently readable, and with touches of humour, this is nevertheless a serious attempt – one of the first in English – to map out a distinctively Welsh literary landscape.

Katie Gramich's fascinating introduction situates Allen Raine's last novel against its literary background and points to its significance in the Anglo-Welsh tradition and in Welsh women's writing.

£7.95   ISBN 1 870206 29 0

A View across the Valley:
Short Stories by Women from Wales 1850-1950
Edited by Jane Aaron

Stories by
Allen Raine, Dorothy Edwards, Hilda Vaughan,
Brenda Chamberlain, Margiad Evans and others

This rich and diverse collection of twenty short stories
provides an opportunity for the modern reader to discover
a lost tradition of English-language storytelling by women
from Wales, as most of the stories have never been re-
published since their first appearance in print. As well as
being entertaining – and often moving – in themselves, the
stories demonstrate how late nineteenth and early
twentieth–century women contributed to the development
of Welsh culture and identity, although their contribution
has since been forgotten.

The volume also includes a general introduction, and
biographical and textual notes on each author and text.
Jane Aaron is a Professor of English at the University of
Glamorgan, and is a renowned expert on Welsh women's
writing.

£7.95   ISBN 1 870206 35 5

The Small Mine
By Menna Gallie

With an introduction by Jane Aaron

First published in 1962, this novel tells the tale of a young collier's death in a mining accident in Cilhendre, a fictional industrial village in the south Wales Valleys. The story vividly and sympathetically portrays how the Valley community, and in particular the women, struggle to come to terms with the sudden loss, an occurrence with which they are all too familiar. Yet for all its tragic subject-matter, *The Small Mine* also conveys the warmth and gusto of the villagers' lives by means of a witty use of language, which was favourably compared to that of Gwyn Thomas and other male Valleys writers on the first appearance of Menna Gallie's Welsh novels.

Menna Gallie (1920-90) was born and reared in Ystradgynlais, near Swansea. *The Small Mine* is the third of her six novels, and was apparently her personal favourite amongst her works. This new edition in the Honno Classics series includes an introduction by Jane Aaron, Professor of English at the University of Glamorgan.

£8.99   ISBN 1 870206 38 X

ABOUT HONNO

Honno Welsh Women's Press was set up in 1986 by a group of women who felt strongly that women in Wales needed wider opportunities to see their writing in print and to become involved in the publishing process. Our aim is to publish books by, and for, the women of Wales, and our brief encompasses fiction, poetry, children's books, autobiographical writing and reprints of classic titles in English and Welsh.

Honno is registered as a community co-operative and so far we have raised capital by selling shares at £5 a time to over 350 interested women all over the world. Any profit we make goes towards the cost of future publications. We hope that many more women will be able to help us in this way. Shareholders' liability is limited to the amount invested, and each shareholder, regardless of the number of shares held, will have her say in the company and a vote at the AGM. To buy shares or to receive further information about forthcoming publications, please write to Honno, 'Ailsa Craig', Heol y Cawl, Dinas Powys, Bro Morgannwg CF64 4AH.

www.honno.co.uk